JONATH

'I have no plans for anything as soul-destroying as marriage . . .' After one disastrous affair with paediatric specialist Jonathan Paget, Sister Rachel Woods knows only too well that they have no future together. Now she must resist him a second time – for how can there be room for love when he has made medicine his life?

Books you will enjoy
in our Doctor Nurse series:

RING FOR A NURSE by Lisa Cooper
DOCTOR IN THE ANDES by Dana James
DR ARROGANT, MD by Lindsay Hicks
BELOVED ANGEL by Lucinda Oakley
NURSE WESTON'S NEW JOB by Clare Lavenham
CANDLES FOR THE SURGEON by Helen Upshall
THE RELUCTANT ANGEL by Sarah Franklin
NURSE ON NEURO by Ann Jennings
THORN-TREE MIDWIFE by Barbara Perkins
NO DOCTORS, PLEASE by Lydia Balmain
A DEDICATED NURSE by Jean Evans
HEART OF A SURGEON by Alexina Rawdon
SISTER IN A SARONG by Jenny Ashe
SIGH FOR A SURGEON by Lynne Collins
A TIME TO HEAL by Sarah Franklin
NURSE IN WAITING by Janet Ferguson
HEART MURMURS by Grace Read
SNOW SISTER by Kate Ashton
DOCTOR KNOWS BEST by Ann Jennings
CINDERELLA SRN by Anna Ramsay
THE HAPPY WARD by Lisa Cooper
THE SURGEON AT ST PETER'S by Rhona Trezise
MARRYING A DOCTOR by Elizabeth Harrison

JONATHAN PAGET, MD

BY

ELIZABETH PETTY

MILLS & BOON LIMITED
15–16 BROOK'S MEWS
LONDON W1A 1DR

First published in Great Britain 1985
by Mills & Boon Limited

ISBN 0 263 75020 5

Set in 10 on 11 pt Linotron Times
03–0485–51,051

Photoset by Rowland Phototypesetting Ltd
Bury St Edmunds, Suffolk
Made and printed in Great Britain by
Richard Clay (The Chaucer Press) Ltd
Bungay, Suffolk

CHAPTER ONE

IN THE late afternoon the wards were fairly quiet on that section of the orthopaedic floor where Rachel and Sister had just finished checking the drugs cabinet. As Rachel was debating whether she had time to go through the linen cupboard with a junior nurse before five-thirty when the meals began again, the phone on the table in the centre of the corridor rang and Sister, indicating to Rachel to answer it, remarked philosophically, 'Well—at least we managed to finish the drugs, Staff. Who is it?'

'Casualty, Sister. They are sending up a patient just admitted. X-rays show that the pin in her femur has moved. She was in here last year—a Mrs Rowntree—and will be going to surgery on Mr Henson's list in the morning.'

'Rowntree—I remember her. Elderly, and one of Dr Paget's. He was registrar here then, of course. Look it up and see if I'm right.'

Rachel reached for the records folders and ran her finger down the columns, very conscious of the jolt to her nerves at the mere mention of Jonathan's name. Yes, there it was and Sister's memory hadn't let her down.

'We'll put her in a side ward for the moment,' she was saying, oblivious of Rachel's reaction to the needless reminder that Jonathan was here only a year ago.

The tall registrar, with his absurd green theatre cap perched on top of his brown hair, would often come to see his patient if he was concerned about him or her, his measured footsteps always recognisable when he came through the swing doors leading to Theatres. Jonathan never sauntered or dithered.

Rachel tried not to think of him too much now because since he had gone to Canada and left a great void in her life, nothing had been the same. She hadn't been able to stop loving him because there had been too much between them to just switch off; but she was living with it.

Sister had disappeared into her office, and as a patient was wheeled along the shining grey corridor from X-Ray, Rachel called a second-year nurse to help her back into bed while she checked that everything was ready for the new patient coming to Number Six.

There were two more emergency admissions before she was free to go off duty, both young and male, and both casualties from motor-bike accidents—an almost daily happening on that floor. So it was late when she knocked on the door of Sister's office and only then did Sister comment on her impending holiday.

'You're off for two weeks, Staff? Where are you going? Somewhere exotic?'

'Oh, no . . .' Rachel said, smiling across the table, and Sister Benson thought, not for the first time, that her once junior nurse had developed into a very attractive young woman since her first appearance on the wards as a rather slight girl, just out of school and as nervous as the rest of the student nurses in their unfamiliar uniforms and minute white caps which were always falling off or over their eyes.

Now Rachel was her right hand and although she might be losing her soon she wasn't going to tell her that today. Rachel's dark eyes, ready smile and sensitive features were aligned to a caring personality which made her popular with patients and staff alike, and her petite figure held more strength than some of the more solid nurses.

'I'm going home for the first week,' Rachel told her.

'Oh, yes—your parents have a farm, don't they, in Wales?'

'A small sheep farm. But it is lovely there—and so peaceful. Then I'm off to Scotland for a week, to stay with Heather.'

'Oh, yes. You two were flatmates—and she's now married to Dr McKay. I heard that she's pregnant . . .'

'Very much so,' Rachel replied smilingly.

'Well, I just hope you aren't called on to act as midwife during your stay—but knowing Heather she will be very organised about the whole thing. Give them our regards and have a good rest.'

'Thank you, Sister.'

As Rachel left the main building and came out into the evening sunshine, the tensions began to slip away. She was free for two whole weeks and it was a wonderful feeling. As she crossed the lawns under the great cedar trees from which the hospital took its name, inevitably Jonathan re-entered her mind—but that was the past and there was nothing she could do about it any more. Now she felt tired and needed the peace and serenity of the green meadows and hillsides of her home in South Wales. Before she set off for her Scottish holiday they would have wrought their own miracle, as always, and she would return to Great Cedars able to cope once more with the next stage in her career.

A week later, Rachel was driving her small car along the shores of Loch Ness in Scotland when suddenly it began to rain soft golden drops, falling through hazy sunshine. She stopped to join a few other tourists parked by the lakeside, all of them gazing out across that mysterious water and wondering if that legendary monster said to be lurking in those murky depths was real or not. Rachel decided that she could easily be persuaded that it was so, especially now that the huge lake looked menacing as the rain clouds darkened the water.

Flexing her aching shoulders, she glanced quickly in her mirror and saw that she needed to renew her lipstick. Then, running a comb through her softly curling dark hair, she decided to push on to Inverness, already sign-posted. It had been a very long drive from the Gretna Green hotel, just inside the Scottish border, where she had stayed the night on her way north, and it was the first time she had attempted anything like the mammoth drive from her home in the Welsh hills. Her parents had both tried to persuade her to travel by train to Scotland, but she had been adamant.

'I'll be fine,' she assured them. 'I like driving.' But in reality she had longed for the escapism, for time to think, time to find herself once more. Changes were in the pipeline career-wise, but she didn't yet know what they were.

One last glance at the lake saw it transformed. There was a rainbow spanning it entirely and the sun shimmered across its surface, golden and sparkling, dispelling the gun-metal grey mistiness and shining through the autumn tints of golden leaves on the trees, which grew along its banks, making them scintillate as they trembled in the breeze; creating a scene of such mesmeric beauty that Rachel's breath caught in her throat. She had driven through the Grampian mountains earlier in the day during a freak snowstorm, which had been quite frightening, and there was snow on Ben Nevis already, cold and fearsome; but now this . . .

Her watch showed it to be almost four o'clock and Inverness only thirty miles or so away. Switching on the engine, she was relieved to hear it responding normally; there had been one or two anxious moments when it seemed to rebel over the last few miles.

Pulling out on to the highway once more, she was

soon caught up in the traffic, and the road, narrowing slightly, needed all her concentration. In front, a huge fish-transporter with foreign lettering on the side, obviously on its way to collect a consignment of mackerel, was commanding more than its share of the road, which cautioned her to slow down and take extra care. She thought longingly of the safety and comfort of the seat in a railway carriage she had so impulsively dispensed with. She was exhausted now and it needed an effort of will to concentrate as the roads into Inverness became even more congested.

She drove into the town, crowded with coaches and heavy traffic in the late afternoon, its pavements packed with shoppers. Edging her way through towards the bridge, she remembered that Heather had said turn left before the bridge over the river. Well, there it was ahead. Fortunately she was in the right lane already and could relax for a moment to appreciate the castle on the hill standing sentinel, beautiful with the golden autumn sunshine floodlighting its grey walls.

The road along by the river would lead her to Heather and Jeff's house. Rachel drove slowly, passing a fisherman knee-deep in the water, his line cast hopefully, patiently waiting for that tug which might mean a salmon for supper. There was a cool breeze as she unwound the window, whipping the river into little wavelets. She would love to have stopped for a while by the grassy banks, but the houses were in sight now and she must look for Riverslea—and Heather or Jeff . . .

Her friend had been looking out for the small red car and was at the white gate, opening it for her to drive in. No one could mistake that copper head, bronzed even more as the sun caught it, Rachel thought happily as Heather stood waiting on the lawn, looking huge with rosy pregnancy. Both girls' faces portrayed their absolute delight at meeting again after so long.

Heather's perceptive green eyes scrutinised Rachel keenly as she unwound her legs and got out of the driving seat.

'You're thinner,' she commented as she hugged her.

'Oh—just a bit, perhaps,' Rachel laughed gaily. 'I can't say the same about you though. But you do look absolutely marvellous. Oh—it's so good to see you!'

'You too, love. Come on into the house. You must be longing for a cup of tea. What on earth made you drive all the way up here? Jeff was speechless when he knew you were coming right from Wales too . . .'

'I enjoy driving and I wanted to be on my own for a while.'

'You and the hoards of other drivers on the motorways—some of them quite suicidal. Very cosy, when you could have relaxed in the train. Well, you know best, honey, but it must have been endless.'

'The last three hours did rather,' Rachel admitted, 'but I had a good night's rest at Gretna. Oh, what a lovely house!' she exclaimed as they went into the blue carpeted hall, bright with autumn flowers in a tall copper jug.

'Is that the one you bought with my cheque?' she asked, stopping to admire it.

Heather nodded. 'It looks perfect on that oak table, doesn't it? I love it. Leave your bag here. We'll take it up when you're ready. Tea first, I think.'

She led the way into the charming kitchen. 'Are you hungry or shall we eat later?'

'I'm not hungry. What time does Jeff get back from the hospital?'

'He is taking a few days off,' Heather told her, 'and gone to do some fishing in the Highlands, so hopefully we shall have a nice fat salmon at the weekend. Which is why I'm so glad to have you to stay. We can natter all we want because I'm dying to catch up on all the newsy gossip at Great Cedars. It *is* lovely to have you,' she ended, a wistful note in her voice. 'I do miss the Cedars. The routine—well, all of it, I suppose; though I wouldn't change a thing and it's been a marvellous year, and now with the baby almost here too . . .'

'You worked part-time at the hospital when you arrived here, didn't you?'

'Yes—it was quite hectic most of the time because I was mobile and filled in where I was most needed. It brought in a few shekels though, which helped a lot because we did take up a higher mortgage than we intended on the house. But it's going to be so worth it, in the long run. Jeff is happy and is very popular at the hospital, as you can imagine. We both love it here.'

'So do I,' Rachel said enthusiastically. 'Here, let me carry that,' she ended, taking the tray from Heather and going with her into the sitting-room which overlooked the river, the bay windows catching the last of the setting sun.

Conversation needed no stimulus as confidences were exchanged and later, when Rachel went up to her room, she stood at the window looking out over a rambling garden filled with colour and edged with trees. Queen Elizabeth roses still clambered up the wall, unafraid, for the present, of the snow and icy winds which would later sweep in from the mountains when winter set in.

'If you lean out you can see the castle on the hill,' Heather commented as she came in and sat down on the bed. 'Very historic here, isn't it?'

'Very. I saw it as I drove by. Where is the hospital? Far?'

'Oh, no. Just the other side of town. Quite within reach when I rush off to the maternity wing.'

'How long? Four weeks?'

'Three, if I'm on time. I can't wait!'

'Yes,' Rachel said wistfully, 'I'd be impatient too. Excited?'

'Ecstatically happy—and quite excited too. We didn't plan it yet, of course.' She giggled reminiscently. 'When Jeff recovered from the shock, he didn't mind too much either.' Her face sobered. 'Rachel, there's something I must tell you,' she said quietly.

'I thought there might be,' Rachel commented perceptively. 'You were going on a bit and you always did that when there was something on your mind. It must be serious if it can't wait. Can I help?'

She sat down beside her friend on the bed and waited, holding against her one of the warm sweaters she had just taken from her case. 'What is it? Tell me.'

'Jonathan's back.'

'Jonathan . . .!' Her voice faltered as she echoed his name. Rachel looked down at her clenched hands around the white sweater. 'When?' She shivered with shock.

'Last week. He phoned Jeff from Prestwick Airport when he got off the plane. We had no idea until then. It just came out of the blue . . .'

Rachel's eyes searched her friend's face; the pain rushing back agonisingly, darkening the pupils as she absorbed the news.

'Prestwick? You mean he came here?'

Heather nodded slowly. 'I didn't know how to tell you. We weren't sure how you would feel about seeing him again, so Jeff thought this fishing trip might be an alternative, to give you time . . .'

'Oh, Heather, you're not trying to tell me that he's coming back here?'

Heather nodded. 'At the weekend. You don't mind too much, do you?' she ended helplessly.

'Mind?' Rachel couldn't keep the hollow note from her voice as she echoed her words. How could she admit that hearing his name had sent shock waves along all the nerves of her spine, undermining the stronghold she had built around her frayed emotions, which was already threatening to crumble. And she had come here to finally dismiss him from her mind . . .

Then the concern on Heather's face as she gazed at her helped bring Rachel back to reality. It was going to be up to her. Heather could well do without this eruption, none of which was her fault, to spoil things for her at this time.

'So—they've gone fishing,' she commented idiotically, between humour and the tears clamouring for release. How dare he do this to her now, when she had looked forward so much to this break away from all the pressures? A thought struck her.

'Is he alone?'

'Yes.'

'So what happened to Cheryl?'

'We didn't ask.'

'He—isn't married then?'

'Obviously not. He may have spoken of it to Jeff while they've been away, I don't know.'

'But why didn't you phone or something? I wouldn't have come.'

'Jonathan wouldn't let us tell you in case you changed your mind.' Heather still looked very unhappy. 'I'm sorry, love, it wasn't part of our plans, you know that. But he was Jeff's buddy, and he did so enjoy seeing him again.'

'Of course. But I wouldn't have come, you know,' Rachel said positively, aware that her heartbeats had accelerated almost to the point of breathlessness. Emotion did that to her—suppressed emotion—but there was still time. She need not be here when he got back. It would be an impossible situation. In the same house, encountering Jonathan's concentrated gaze each time she had to speak to him—his look compelling her to reveal in her brown eyes that she still loved him; that he could still submerge her whole being if he chose. She would never give him the opportunity for that to happen again. She could always leave before the two men returned from their trip after all, because she knew she wouldn't be able to repress her feelings about Jonathan completely, and it would only prove embarrassing to all of them. So she just wouldn't be here.

Immersed in her own thoughts, she looked up to see that Heather was still feeling anything but happy. She hadn't intruded on Rachel's cogitation, leaving her to absorb the shock of knowing that he was back, but she was looking miserable about the whole thing now.

Impulsively, Rachel stretched out her hand to give Heather's arm a quick squeeze.

'Don't worry about it. We have until the weekend and I can always go to a hotel for a couple of days.'

'You can't do that!' Heather was adamant. 'Oh, don't you see, it would only make things worse! Besides, you're here at our invitation—it's part of your holiday and heaven knows, you must need it. Jeff wanted us two to be together for a time. We'll work something out. After all, the four of us were always so compatible; couldn't we be again? Please . . .'

'That was before Cheryl came on the scene,' Rachel said shortly. 'I can't see him—it's impossible. We weren't even speaking to each other when he went off to Canada, remember?'

'Of course I remember, and what it did to you emotionally. You were shattered . . . But you stuck it out. And after a while the hoo-ha died down and you no longer thought everyone was feeling sorry for you. Now you can quietly show Jonathan that we can still all be friends—and the past is just that, relegated.'

'Oh, Heather, I can't do that—don't you see?

Because it will never be over, not for me. He was, and is, the only man who . . .' Rachel turned her head away to hide her emotion then.

'I think I know,' Heather said gently. 'It really was much more than just an affair between you. You really loved him, didn't you? I thought it had to be that serious, which is why it's so difficult to understand how he could have acted the way he did.'

'I can't talk about it. Sorry . . .' Rachel's voice trembled.

'Okay, love. Finish your unpacking. I'll go and heat the casserole and get some fresh fruit marinading for supper. After all, we do have another three days of comparative calm on our own before we need face up to this one,' Heather said practically, heaving her cumbersome body off the bed.

Rachel went to the chest of drawers to put her things away; then, on pulling out one of the smaller drawers, saw that it contained handkerchiefs and socks and a few personal things, most of which were initialled J. He must have been using this room then. The sight of a small leather note-book case made her catch her breath. She knew what she would see inside it because she had given it to Jonathan last year. It used refills—and he still had it.

Opening it, she saw the inscription 'J from R' in gold lettering and impulsively put it against her cheek, the smell of the leather mingling with his own particular male scent. Her throat contracted in the emotion of the moment as she remembered the night she had given it to him. The promise of a shared future was so much a part of her life then that there were no fears when Dr Cheryl Summers appeared on the scene, having come over from Canada on a six months' exchange scheme.

It was natural that Jonathan should want to show

Cheryl around his beloved Bath and Gloucester and the glorious Cotswolds, so historically English, when Rachel was either on duty or studying for her finals. She trusted him completely—and had been the last to realise that there was more to it than that. Afterwards, when he had told her about his research grant at the same hospital to which Cheryl would return, it all became clear.

'It will be for one or two years probably,' he had said, 'but it's something I can't turn down.' And he had gone on to explain about the breakthrough in bone marrow disease in children which he wanted to research before he specialised.

She hadn't really listened. Her ego took the blow, while she herself backed out as quietly as she did most things, simply going home to Wales for a few days so that she wouldn't have to see him again before he flew out.

In her suffering she had thought she was doing the only possible thing—to leave the field wide open for his new love and release him from any responsibility he may feel towards herself.

When she returned from Wales to Great Cedars, Jonathan and Dr Summers had flown out the previous day.

Carefully closing the drawer Rachel went down to the kitchen, having reached a decision. But Heather forestalled her.

'I've been thinking. It's just possible that Jonathan may decide to go off down to London, or even to his parents in Bath when they get back from their trip.'

'I've been thinking too,' Rachel said thoughtfully. 'There's a hotel just across the river. I could go there if he decides to stay—and we could still see each other . . .'

Heather closed the oven door and straightened up,

her hands pressed to the small of her back. 'There's nothing to be gained by running away. It never solved anything. You'll have to see Jonathan.'

Rachel began to dry the cups she had just washed. She was thinking hard, her brow furrowed.

'You're right,' she admitted, making a new and instant decision. 'I've never run away from anything before, so why now? I shall show him that I'm over him; that he was one of my mistakes. Regrettable, but true, and I shall behave beautifully. So you don't have to worry about it.'

Heather breathed an audible sigh of relief. 'Thank goodness for that,' she said fervently. 'So what about uncorking that bottle of wine in the fridge? I think I've got my appetite back.'

'I'm sorry, did I give you a bad time?' Rachel asked, stretching her hand for the corkscrew.

'Well, let's say I've had rather an apprehensive day,' Heather said lightly, glad to see that Rachel was ready to smile again.

But in fact it was Rachel now who felt some apprehension, wondering how she could carry out her promise to behave normally when the two men returned. Already her heart was beating wildly at even the thought of Jonathan coming in through that door. Where would the bravado she had just voiced be when she saw those teasing, even mocking, hazel eyes testing her out to see how much effect they were having, once more exerting his will over hers? It was almost prophetic, unless she kept to her decision to leave him in no doubt about her feelings where he was concerned.

The next two days were thoroughly enjoyable ones. They walked by the river until Heather had exercised enough and talked as they used to, recapturing the closeness they had shared at Great Cedars. On Friday Rachel drove them both into town for lunch and some weekend shopping, to Heather's delight, as she could no longer slide behind the wheel of the car in the garage.

While Heather was putting away the salads and fruit bought in town, Rachel decided to slip up to her room and gift-pack the tiny baby garments she had surreptitiously paid for while Heather went on out to the car. Smocking was back in vogue and the clothes were exquisitely embroidered. She felt oddly emotional as she tied them with baby ribbons in the 'new arrival' paper.

As they were alone both girls had decided not to change and now, glancing in the mirror, Rachel felt rather glad that she could keep on the cosy cream sweater and beige pleated skirt she had worn that day. The beige soft leather boots to match were one of her extravagances from the previous year. It was cold tonight and the central heating was not yet switched on inside the house.

A comb through her hair and a touch of lipstick, and finally a spray of 'Je Reviens' perfume completed her preparations for a meal which already promised to be good. And now she was feeling really hungry. They were having grilled gammon steak tonight, with pineapple. It used to be their treat on pay-days at the hospital and would probably start them reminiscing, so she was humming as she went down the stairs. But Rachel stopped dead when the sound of car wheels crunched on the gravel outside.

Heather heard them too and came into the hall as car lights splayed the window in the growing dusk.

'Good heavens, it's them! Why on earth didn't they phone?' she exclaimed, glancing up at Rachel, her hand pressed to her mouth, transfixed on the fourth stair.

'I thought you said tomorrow . . .' she murmured, as she came on down very slowly. 'What now?'

'Don't worry, we can find something for their supper,' Heather said, quickly going forward to open the door.

The last thing Rachel had taken into consideration was what they would eat. Her heart was beating wildly as she clung to the banister, but the next moment Heather was being enveloped in her husband's arms, as far as it was possible, as she gasped, 'What happened? Were you longing for some home comforts? A bit spartan was it, up there in that old wooden hut?'

'We had a heavy snowstorm actually, and decided to cut it short,' he answered with a grin. 'I *was* missing you a bit before that, but we got a couple of fair-sized salmon. Why, hallo there, Rachel. I didn't see you.'

Now it was her turn for a hug against his smelly woollen sweater and she voiced her question. 'Where is Jonathan?'

'He's unloading.' Then softly, looking into her face, Jeff said, 'It *is* okay, isn't it? I mean . . .'

'Of course. Let me take those things.'

She turned to hang up his oilskins and waders while he went back for more. Her mind was tuned in now as if she was dealing with an emergency, and then Jonathan was standing there on the hall carpet, feet apart, regarding her with something like disbelief—his eyebrows raised quizzically.

'It's true then. I wasn't quite sure if Jeff was pulling my leg or not. I thought you might have left.'

'Why?' she asked coolly, surprised at herself.

'Oh—a number of reasons. How are you, Rachel?'

'Fine, thanks.'

'Aren't you glad to see me?'

'You're no longer important to me, Jonathan. I'm not particularly, as it happens.'

He regarded her for a second or so from under half-closed eyelids while she forced herself to meet his still curious expression bravely. He seemed to take every part of her body into that one long, sustained look, before he said softly, 'So, we're playing it that way, are we?'

Before she could give him the reply rising hotly to her lips, Jeff and Heather came in from the kitchen together.

'They both need a good hot bath,' she remarked, wrinkling up her nose. 'We'll eat when they've scrubbed up and smell more wholesome. I should think they've slept in those clothes for the past few days and Jeff hasn't even shaved! Come and give me a hand, love. Fortunately, I can stretch the meal.'

The two men disappeared upstairs, their feelings hurt by the lack of gratitude shown for their catch, but promising not to be too long. Their voices came floating back down.

Heather closed the grilling oven and turned a flushed face to Rachel before whispering. 'How did it go?'

'Oh—no problems.' Rachel's mouth trembled imperceptibly behind the forced words. 'Nothing's really changed, has it? He looks different though.'

Heather shrugged. 'Having exchanged a white house coat for a filthy sweater, you mean?'

'Should we change?' Rachel asked anxiously.

'Why not? You're on holiday and it's quite an occasion after all.'

'Right, you go on up first while I keep an eye on the kitchen and do the table.'

'Oh, thanks,' Heather said gratefully. 'I think I might just squeeze into that green shapeless thing I showed you.'

Rachel felt a desperate need for solitude, just for a few minutes. Her head was aching a little and her heart behaving erratically. Emotions needed to be expressed and she was bottling her own very tightly, even pushing in the cork so that they couldn't escape. There had to be a resultant headache.

She was terribly conscious of Jonathan's presence in the house. Much too close for comfort and already threatening to sink her resistance with his power over her. If he thought, for one moment, that he could pick up where he had left off, go back to the time before Cheryl came, then he underestimated the depth of hurt and even bitterness, as well as a damaged ego, which had torn at her heart-strings after she knew they were going to Canada together. Without even an explanation. Not that she had given him an opportunity for one; for he had become angry and her flight to Wales had only made things worse.

Was he going back? Or was he here now to stay?

She finished the table and had stood back to check that everything was perfect when she felt, rather than saw, him. He was outlined in the soft glow of the table lamp in the doorway, watching her.

'Oh . . .!' she couldn't prevent the exclamation of surprise escaping, and his expression was disconcerting to say the least. How long had he been there?

'You're thinner,' he said in a low voice, coming into the room, 'and still a perfectionist, I see. Everything has still to be in place, hasn't it, Rachel?' He regarded her thoughtfully. 'Haven't you yet learned to be a little more flexible?'

He had changed into a cream roll-necked silky sweater and black pants, his face and lean figure just as she remembered. Even his fingers on the back of a chair were reminders of the number of times she had watched them while he was working in theatre and she one of the duty nurses. She knew the strength of those hands —and their gentleness too.

A sob caught in her throat, utterly without warning, which was infuriating, and brushing past him she said angrily, 'I'm not interested in your opinion, Jonathan, so just keep it to yourself. I'm only here now for Heather's sake. I certainly never wanted to see you again, believe me. I'm just sorry you had to choose this particular time to come back. I wanted to leave before you returned.'

'Then why didn't you?' he asked softly, his voice just audible as she crossed the hall.

CHAPTER TWO

UPSTAIRS in her room behind a closed door, Rachel fought to control the emotions which once again, by his mere physical presence, Jonathan had set into tumultuous motion. How dared he come back here? And why did she let him do this to her? she asked herself, refuting all the resolutions she had so blithely made that never again would she be this vulnerable and love one man so much that without him she was only half a person.

But just now he had come so close—too close, and the trembling had begun in all her limbs. He had been near enough to touch her; the flecks in his eyes mesmerisingly part of the expression which had always wakened her desires; that unresisting longing for the feel of his arms around her, his hands on her back as she moved into them, before that moment when their mouths clung together. Those were the memories she had lived with, tortured herself with, over the past year. And for what? To let him do it to her all over again?

Oh no . . . She wouldn't ever become that vulnerable again. It was just the shock of seeing him, out of the blue like that. It was enough to shake anyone.

When they were alone sometime, he would know what she really thought of him; hear all those suppressed and angry thoughts which she had never divulged to anyone. Perhaps it would devastate his ego a little to know that he wasn't the answer to every woman's prayer and that she was certainly not ready to fall back into his arms again. Now now. Not ever. Because, sadly, there was no more trust between them and without that there could be nothing.

Having reminded herself of this, she wondered, adversely, why she was letting him disturb her so much. Crossing to the dressing-table, she stared assessingly into the mirror at the pale oval of her face and dark eyes, large and with a haunted expression which belied her own assessment of her state of mind.

If only she had gone to the hotel, as she had intended, when she first knew that he was back. It was too late now, of course. He would know that it was because of him. And she had to think of Heather's feelings too.

She drew a deep breath, resolving to play this in the only possible way; convincingly enough to show Jonathan that he no longer interested her and certainly had no hold on her emotions. It shouldn't be too difficult, if she set out to do it. It wasn't likely that they would be alone during the weekend, and after that she could always leave a day or two earlier.

Jeff's voice came up to her, sending her to open the door.

'Rachel, are you coming down? It's Martini time!'

'Be right there . . .' Somehow she managed to channel her voice to his wavelength. No one could even suspect the emotional reaction she had just passed through, she thought, as she repaired her make-up and ran a comb through her hair. Another quick spray of perfume and, pushing her feet into high-heeled cream sandals this time, which added height, she went down to join them.

Heather looked just a little anxiously at her as she went into the lounge, but by then Rachel's smile was back and she avoided looking at Jonathan.

'Ice and lemon?' Jeff asked casually, perhaps the least sensitive to the atmosphere which threatened to erupt into a tense situation unless his two guests played it down.

But because Jonathan was behaving perfectly, some

of the tension evaporated. The four of them had always been so good together; something of it still came through, and Jeff was asking, man-like, 'How long is supper going to be, darling? We're starving.'

Heather raised her eyebrows. 'It's ready,' she said patiently, 'and waiting for you. Just give me a minute.'

'I'll help.' Rachel followed her to the kitchen, glass in hand, hoping that no one detected the relief in her voice. She insisted on getting the plates and dishes from the warm drawer of the cooker. 'I'm sure it's more comfortable if you don't have to bend double,' she commented significantly.

'But isn't it typical,' Heather grumbled gently, 'that even having a doctor for one's husband, doesn't make him appreciate the fact that most things take a little longer to achieve? One feels so huge! I'm sure he doesn't realise just how close he is to becoming a father. Are you okay, love?' Rachel's paleness hadn't gone unnoticed.

'Fine. And this really does smell delicious. Shall I light the candles?'

'Please. The table looks lovely. Thanks. I'm so glad you're here.' She finished impulsively, 'Let's make it a fun evening.'

Rachel smiled sympathetically. 'If that's your mood, we will,' she promised, silently calling up all her reserves for Heather's sake. She even met Jonathan's tentative, questing half-smile as he came into the room with one of her own, the corners of her mouth lifting slightly. And when he held her chair as she sat down, her voice was soft as she thanked him.

He really was going out of his way to be charming, she knew, watching him sitting opposite and facing her, and wished she could stop an inner trembling which was now making itself felt.

His easy manner conveyed his delight at being back in

England and together like this. He looked significantly across the table at her but Rachel presumed not to notice and busied herself gathering up the dishes, so that Heather needn't get up.

Inevitably, Great Cedars came into the conversation and it fell to Rachel, being the only one of the four still connected with it, to bring the others up to date about personnel and developments there, especially the new wings which had been recently added.

'And Rachel says that old Fergus has retired at last,' Heather broke in. 'He was an old dear, but such a fuddy-duddy, wasn't he? Two new surgeons in Cardiology, aren't there, Rachel?'

'Mmm. Over three months ago.'

Jonathan glanced up from the orange he was dissecting and looked right at her as he told her calmly, 'I too shall probably be returning to Great Cedars next month. Did you know?' he asked lazily, obviously not caring whether she knew or not.

'I'm surprised,' she answered coolly. 'I should have thought you would be going back to Canada.'

'No. My year's research is behind me and I need to take up where I left off, Rachel.'

Her head went up like a startled fawn. 'That isn't usually possible.'

'I wouldn't say that. I've only been away a year and it's proved invaluable. I wouldn't have missed it for anything.'

'Good,' she commented drily, but thinking to herself, not for me—unless I too learn something from it.

'More wine?' Jeff asked, and she held her glass for him to fill again, feeling a sudden need for it to dull the aching pain somewhere in her body. She must try to relax, ease the tautened nerves and muscles which were building up into a knot of unbearable tension again, in spite of her brave resolutions. The strange part was that neither Heather nor Jeff appeared to notice anything unusual. Jonathan did, she knew. But only because it involved him.

Bedtime came at last and Heather went up first, after which Rachel, too, crawled gratefully up to her room, leaving the men to talk.

This had been Jonathan's bed before he went off on that fishing trip. Heather must have tactfully moved his things into the room designated for a nursery. Rachel, turning her head into the pillow, willing sleep to come before Jonathan came upstairs, couldn't resist a little smile as she imagined him falling asleep surrounded by a frieze of Beatrix Potter animals wandering off into the hills of the Lake District, his clothes folded into the drawers of the white-painted furniture which stood in readiness for the small son or daughter soon to arrive on the scene.

She wouldn't have minded having that room but Heather hadn't even suggested it. It must be wonderful to have a baby of one's own, if it was conceived and born of love. How could one ever forget just when that baby was made between two people? If it were hers and Jonathan's she would know. Longingly, she dreamed of how it would be—then, almost immediately, erased it from her mind. The last thing he wanted, he had told her firmly, was to be a father—in any sense of the word. Lover or nothing. Maybe none of his relationships would ever be the lasting kind.

How well she had known him? Really known him? The real man, ambitious, calculating, always with an end in view. Perhaps using every liaison as a stepping-stone to what lay beyond. Was she wronging him? Had Cheryl not filled his need? Was that why he had left her behind? Or was she coming over later? Was his just a thirst for knowledge perhaps? Must nothing stand in the way of his aim to heal people, especially children, who were previously incurable? Must he shut everything else out, because of it?

Tossing restlessly, Rachel had almost decided that tonight must be a sleepless one when she unconsciously slept, only to waken when a shaft of early sun fell across her face and she blinked in the weak strength of the day's first sunbeam.

She threw back the covers and went to the window. The house and garden were silent. There was a mist over the mountains, towards the Highlands, and it looked like a good day ahead. The trees were changing colour rapidly now, their bright golden leaves dropping in solitary fashion on to the green lawn. She thought she might go out and along by the river for an early walk and, taking her towel and pulling on her housecoat, she walked silently along to the bathroom.

As she was about to return to her room after turning to close the bathroom door, she gave a gasp at the unexpected sight of Jonathan, his bare legs and feet firmly planted to bar her way. He wore, as she discovered when her eyes ascended to the rest of him, a short brown towelling robe and, she was almost sure, nothing under it.

Caught off guard, she felt the heat and confusion which spread through her body as he made no attempt to move out of her way.

'Please move, Jonathan . . .' she whispered tersely, looking up into the lazy depths of his tigerish eyes. The tip of his tongue protruded between his well-shaped lips and she saw the gleam of white teeth and knew that he was in one of his teasing moods.

Thrusting off his restraining hand on her arm, she tried to push past him but his grip was meant to keep her there, and now he was grinning broadly as he bent to whisper softly, 'Hi—you always did look wonderful in the morning, honey. But you're up early, aren't you?'

'So are you,' she muttered, pushing past him and going quickly into her room, closing the door as quietly as possible.

But Jeff and Heather, even if they heard her door, would never intrude, probably surmising that she and Jonathan had resolved their differences and simply taken up where they had left off, which they were hoping would happen.

A half-sob caught in her throat Only she herself knew that it could never be that way again between them. It was a shattering blow from which she hadn't quite recovered. She dared not try to answer the question she asked herself. Was she completely over Jonathan? Because the answer which came up was not the practical one. And instead of going forward, able to cope now without him, she was letting it all start up again, heading for the same disastrous climax as before. Unless she was strong and meant what she said. Because, it seemed, her thoughts contradicted her words over and over.

Why didn't she just get in the car and drive south and back to the small sheep farm in the hills, with no entanglements or traumas? She would suggest it to Heather when she came down for breakfast.

But Heather wasn't feeling too well. Rachel took over in the kitchen and after breakfast the two men decided to take off for another day's fishing. Trout was rising down-river and this was too much to resist.

'It is my last day before I become submerged again—you don't mind, do you?' Jeff had asked tentatively, giving Heather that little-boy look which every wife knows.

'Of course not,' she said good-naturedly. 'I know you can't wait to get those rods going again—or is it nets this time?'

They had driven off like two schoolboys on a picnic

and Rachel had then insisted that Heather sit on the patio with her feet up while she weeded the borders and ran the mower over the lawns for the last time that year, Jeff being the world's worst gardener and leaving it to his wife to achieve the lovely colours which had welcomed Rachel on the first day.

Later she made coffee for them both, bringing it out into the autumn sunshine and sitting with Heather, who looked very tired. They were good for each other and had been friends from their first week at Great Cedars when, as raw student nurses, they had donned their white caps and print dresses, nervously sitting, scared and unsure, through their first anatomy lecture. At the end of the three months they couldn't either of them see themselves getting through the first year, and never expected to reach the end of a second, but they had both emerged with flying colours as State Registered nurses at the end of it all.

'Tell me, Rachel, how do you feel about Jonathan now that you've been with each other again?' she asked anxiously. 'Last night you seemed quite good together, then this morning you didn't say two words to each other. Is it hopeful, or just not on?'

'Definitely, not on,' Rachel said positively. 'We're calling a truce, that's all. It doesn't bother you, does it? Or Jeff?'

'No. But I wish I had a psychology degree—I think I'd find the behaviour of both of you rather intriguing.'

'Don't cramp my style,' Rachel warned, 'or I could feel emotionally restrained and then it might show. Have you any idea how long he is staying here?'

Heather shook her head laughingly. 'None at all. So you aren't getting rid of him that easily, I'm afraid!'

While Heather went upstairs to rest, Rachel prepared a cheesecake, her thoughts busy, remembering how Jonathan had kept coming into her mind on the long drive up here. Perhaps that should have given her some warning. If only she had listened to her intuition, she would have had some indication of an impending meeting. But how could she have foreseen that he would actually be here, in this house with her?

And it wasn't over yet. For she couldn't just desert Heather, who obviously needed someone around to lend a hand. And when she did go—and Jonathan came to Great Cedars again, if he did—what was going to happen to all her ready-made ideas? Surely that would leave the ball very definitely in her court? She would have no alternative but to leave the Cedars and start again in some other hospital—but the Cedars was almost like home to her now. Her flat in the nurses' home was a special place. She didn't want to leave.

When she had taken Heather a cup of tea, Rachel had a bath and went back to her room, writing some postcards to other staff at the hospital and to her parents.

As she was changing into a classically plain cream dress, zipping up the back, she heard the car tyres outside on the gravel and her hand stayed suspended in mid-air. A shaft of apprehension, balanced fairly with a glow of latent excitement, shot through her body. Then she heard his voice, his deep laugh in the hall, as he and Jeff recounted something to Heather who was now obviously feeling better and ready to cope again, for she joined in their laughter.

Almost savagely Rachel knotted an emerald green scarf around her neck and, thrusting her feet into fashion sandals, went to the door. But when she heard him coming up the stairs, two at a time, she closed it again and waited.

Why, oh why did she let him affect her this way? Her colour had heightened; her heart was thumping in her breast. She felt a real compulsion to be near him again, which she had to accept as proof that nothing had changed. Now, though, it had become, for the next few days at least, a game of pretence. Because he must never know that he could just walk back into her life and that her defences weakened this way.

When Jonathan left his room for the bathroom, she opened her door and went down to help Heather. But she knew that she was waiting impatiently for him to appear. She was already obsessed with the need, the longing, to be near him.

Yet Jonathan thought she seemed even more withdrawn than previously, so he deliberately drew her into the conversation throughout the delicious meal. And when Jeff asked how the girls had spent their day, he raised his eyebrows to give her a concentrated look when Heather replied truthfully, 'I sat on the patio and watched Rachel working in the garden; then she insisted on sending me to bed for the afternoon.'

'That's no way to treat a guest,' Jeff commented teasingly.

'She also made the blackcurrant cheesecake,' Heather told him. 'And Rachel isn't exactly a guest, is she? But she should be getting out more, seeing the country around the town. It is supposed to be her holiday, after all.'

'It *is* a holiday,' Rachel protested, her face flushing as she felt Jonathan's gaze on her. Even now, he knew only too well the effect he was having as he sat watching her.

Rachel knew then that there was no way she could go through an evening like this, but what was the alternative? So it was a great relief to hear Jeff remind Heather that he had promised to take Jonathan to see a colleague after supper, and didn't she think she should go to bed early?

The pressure was off, for tonight, at least.

On Sunday the two men were going off for a round of golf and lunch at the club, again much to Rachel's relief.

'Of course, this wouldn't happen if you weren't here,' Jeff excused them both, grinning delightedly.

'Neither would we spend Sunday apart if I wasn't in this rotund state,' Heather broke in. 'But as it is, we won't mind some time on our own today.'

She looked to Rachel to back her up.

'If you can get into my car, I'll take us along to look at the castle,' Rachel suggested.

'I can try. That's a great idea. And tomorrow I have to go for a check at the hospital so you really must do something interesting, Rachel. The days are flying by and you haven't been anywhere.'

'Tomorrow? I'm free. Let's do something together,' Jonathan broke in. 'Lunch? Anything. You're on holiday, remember. What would you like to do, Rachel?'

When she made no reply, he shrugged his shoulders and went to talk to Jeff outside.

'You are making it rather obvious,' Heather commented a little reproachfully.

'I know. I can't help that. I don't want to go out with him. Don't try throwing us together, please, Heather.'

'Okay, love. If that's how it is . . .' Heather said over her shoulder. But she couldn't help noticing the way Rachel was looking after Jonathan's retreating figure as he walked down the crazy-paving path to join Jeff, doing a few last minute things to the car.

And Rachel was seeing Jonathan just as she had so many times over the past year when, unbidden, he came into her mind. His shoulders, bent a little forward because he was usually deep in thought as he walked the hospital corridors in his white coat. Or listening attentively to a patient's answers to his questions or, sometimes, laughing with the other doctors; at such times another side of him came into focus.

'Oh, Jonathan,' she whispered, 'we were so right together. What happened? Where did I go wrong?'

The ache in her heart was back. It sapped her energy, making her limbs lethargic as she went up to her room to get something warmer if they were to walk around the castle ramparts. Even she recognised the strain in her own face. Some holiday—when she had so wanted to finally erase him from her mind and make it a new start.

'Rachel Woods!' she said aloud to her image. 'You've got a lot of decision-making ahead. Much better to cut and run from Great Cedars—the lot. And plump for a completely new start somewhere fresh.'

Which gave her something new to think about for the rest of the day.

On Monday morning Jeff left early and breakfast was eaten in the kitchen. Rachel suggested that she should take Heather into the hospital that afternoon. There was no way she wanted to be alone with Jonathan.

'Oh, that's been taken care of.' Heather was adamant. 'Jeff is coming home early for a snack lunch and I'll go back with him. So do something nice today, both of you.'

'I can think of lots of things,' Jonathan said lightly, unable to resist giving Rachel a significant glance. He had an amused gleam in his eyes which she ignored, getting up to start the breakfast dishes.

'Why don't you have your bath?' she suggested, as Heather, still wearing her bulging housecoat, came to help. 'That way you won't have to hurry.'

'Good idea,' Jonathan agreed, taking the tea towel in his hands and waiting for the first cereal dish to emerge from the washing-up suds. Rachel was already regretting her suggestion. This wasn't at all what she wanted, to have him standing as close to her as this. Besides, he was looking particularly masculine in his red-checked Canadian cowboy shirt and blue jeans today, a new image completely.

It was building up; her awareness of him. He was so close she could feel his breath on her neck, smell his clean masculinity, bringing back vividly those other times when the scent of his skin had mingled with her own. She closed her eyes, willing the moment of weakness to pass before he had any suspicion of what he was doing to her, deliberately or otherwise.

'Rachel . . .' His voice held the pleading that it had that last time before he left for Canada, when he wanted to talk to her but she had refused to listen. Now he stood with his back against the sink, facing her. 'We have to bring this whole thing into the open. Let's take today—go somewhere and clear the cobwebs. It's the right time, don't you think?' he said seriously.

Angrily she shook off the hand he had slipped under her elbow, gently drawing her towards him. The colour rushed to her face.

'We have nothing to say to each othere, Jonathan. It was all said before you went away, and nothing has changed.'

'Of course it has or I wouldn't be here,' he said roughly, his own irritation rising now. 'Okay, if that's the way you intend playing it we both know where we are.'

He flung the towel down and strode out.

'What other way can there be?' she muttered after his retreating back, as tears welled up and threatened to overflow into the washing-up bowl. So she didn't see the almost irritated glance he threw back over his shoulder before he went out to the garage.

When she was making her bed he came into the house again, so she stayed where she was. Heather came out on to the landing and said she was going down to make coffee.

But within minutes, Jonathan's car started up and disappeared into the avenue. Rachel felt nothing but relief. Now she could go down and enjoy her coffee. Yet, perversely, the house seemed empty without him.

'Jonathan's gone to the garage to get his car checked and doesn't think he'll be back for lunch,' Heather told her.

Rachel grimaced. 'I suppose I should get mine serviced before I drive back on Friday. It did jump a bit when I drove up and sometimes I fancied the steering-wheel jerked a bit.'

'Then of course you must. If Jeff gives the garage a ring they will hurry it up a bit. He always gets priority.'

'He's a doctor, I'm not.'

'Oh, they're very good. I'll talk to him at lunch-time.'

'Well,' Rachel said hesitantly, 'I thought I might drive into the shops and get a few things to take back; and then maybe explore around the hills a bit.'

'By yourself?'

'I like my own company.'

'So you're feeling the need for isolation again,' Heather said tentatively.

'Something like that. And you're going to be tied up at the hospital—unless you would like me to come with you?'

'I'd hate it, frankly. And you'll have all the hospital atmosphere you want when you get back to Cedars.'

'Yes,' Rachel said wistfully. 'If I stay . . . Meanwhile, I'll take myself off into town if you're sure.'

'See you later,' her friend said blithely, a smile lurking in her green eyes as she wondered if Rachel and Jonathan had an assignation somewhere and preferred to keep it secret for the moment. That would be almost too much to hope for. Poor Jonathan, he obviously had a lot of explaining to do before Rachel could ever trust him again.

The small red car started first time and, after an hour's shopping and a snack lunch, Rachel couldn't resist driving out towards the small villages in the lovely autumn sunshine which tipped the trees with unbelievable colour, perfect against the blue-grey of the hills. She wanted to walk up there—quite alone.

With no regard for direction or even how far from town she drove, Rachel followed as the lanes twisted into the countryside and she stopped by the side of a burn to watch the clear water gurgling and hurrying over the clean stones and pebbles and small fish darting under them to hide. Here the colours too were spectacular, rich with the reds and russets of early autumn, the tree branches dripping with golden leaves and red berries and, above, a sky so blue it was like a backcloth that was almost too perfect.

Suddenly she wanted to share it with Jonathan. Balancing precariously on one of the larger, rounded bleached stones, she bent to let the icy water trickle through her fingers, feeling like a child again in the peace of her surroundings. She had no idea where she was; a few cottages dotted about were the only indication that people lived here.

She climbed a little higher and sat watching sheep in the field below and, inevitably, Jonathan came into her mind again, tormenting her with his power over her emotions, his physical nearness that morning, sheer proof that he still had the same magnetism over her.

She had felt the trembling he evoked in her limbs. If he had held her just once he would have known it too. How she had wanted to turn into his waiting arms—and if she had, that first kiss would have been the preliminary to surrender.

Why was she doing this? she thought wearily. How

utterly stupid. Deliberately resurrecting what she had fought against all year. Anger, regret, hurt ego—they had all played a part before she finally put Jonathan behind her.

But now he was back, and all the magic was there—in his eyes, the touch of his hands . . .

She must cut short her holiday and return to Wales and her parents' farm. Besides, it would be easier for Heather if there was one less person to cater for. And Jonathan obviously didn't intend to leave yet.

Today was as good as any. She would drive back now and tell them of her decision.

Rachel was still not thinking rationally when she got the car started again, because she took a small lane which led her through fields and woods and soon became not much more than a track. She had better find somewhere to turn. Perhaps the open gate leading into that field would give her room to back. As she tried to reverse, the engine gave an ominous grunt and died on her. Desperately she tried to get it started, but with no response.

'Oh damn!' she muttered, getting out and lifting the bonnet, which told her nothing. Exasperation and the nagging worry that she was also lost made her curse her own stupidity. That final grunt from the car engine had been unpleasantly loud and she wasn't out of petrol—so the bumpy lane was probably to blame.

Locking the door, she scanned the surrounding countryside. A column of smoke spiralled up from the chimney of a cottage away to her left, it was just possible they might have a telephone.

She began to walk; surely she would reach it soon? Looking back she just hoped that nothing would come round the bend in the track and flatten her car, because it wouldn't be seen in time.

Rachel, who hated incompetence, was guilty of laxity

now in not making sure that her car was properly serviced. She had taken risks she would never have contemplated and it did nothing to improve her state of mind.

It seemed very lonely as she skirted the woods, coming out suddenly to the small cottage standing by itself in a patch of garden with a few vegetables behind.

Some chickens scratched away in the adjoining field and a few scattered toys on the path indicated there were children somewhere; indeed, one was crying inside the cottage. Quite a frightened cry, which she recognised as such. And then, through the open door, came a woman's piercing scream, the kind which can't be prevented from escaping, and recognisable to any nurse or doctor.

The door was open; Rachel reached it quickly, walking straight into a real emergency, taking everything in at a glance.

A woman, in her thirties probably, lay in an unnatural position on the floor with one leg doubled under her. She had screamed when she tried to move, having obviously fallen from the chair which lay overturned on the floor. Like Heather she was heavily pregnant—almost full term.

'Oh God, I knew you'd help me . . .' she sobbed, as Rachel knelt beside her holding the shaking hands firmly.

Rachel knew just how serious it was then. The woman's leg was broken, that was painfully obvious, and she had gone into labour.

Two small girls clung together in a large armchair, their faces tear-stained, both sobbing from sheer fright at the sight of their mother in desperate pain on the floor. Somehow Rachel smiled at them reassuringly.

'Your leg is broken,' she said quietly to the woman. 'I'll get some help, but meanwhile I'll try to make you more comfortable. This has started the baby, hasn't it?'

'Oh . . .' the woman groaned softly. 'Yes, I'm afraid so—it isn't due for another month.'

'All right. Hold on. Just tell me where things are if you can . . .'

Rachel flew upstairs, returning with blankets and pillows, which she placed behind her patient; at least the woman could rest her head now. And there was a telephone and numbers on a pad, thank goodness.

But when Rachel dialled the midwife, who apparently lived only a quarter of an hour away, there was no reply. She left a recorded message before, without hesitation, she dialled 999 and asked for an ambulance.

'Right away, please.'

'Name and address?' the efficient voice at the other end asked patiently.

'Just one moment. Where are we? And your name?'

'McAllister,' the woman on the floor could barely answer. Between bouts of pain she muttered, 'Braillay—turn by the school . . .'

Briefly Rachel explained the situation before going back to kneel beside her patient again. If only she had something to alleviate the pain of the leg—but she knew she dared not touch it, for the bone was already showing white through the torn skin. The ambulancemen would have a temporary plastic splint and should be here soon, she hoped. Her patient seemed to be less frightened now and as the children were quiet too, she went to them. They simply must not stay in the room.

'Do you think you could wait by the gate and come and tell me when a big white car comes down the lane? I'll take care of your mummy—and that would be a real help.'

'Daddy has gone to the market with some sheep,' the elder child told her tearfully.

'Then I expect he'll soon be back, so you could go and look for him to come too, while I make mummy more comfortable. She'll soon feel better—don't worry.'

Trustingly they went out into the garden, hand in hand, and as soon as the door closed Rachel dialled Heather's number to try and make arrangements for her car to be moved. Hopefully she would be home by now. After a few rings a man answered. She had heard Jonathan's voice too many times at the end of a phone wire at the Cedars not to recognise it now and a spasm of uplift settled around her heart region.

'Oh, Jonathan . . .'

'Hi, there—is something wrong?'

Now how on earth had he known that, just from one word?

'Is Heather there?'

'No, she isn't,' he answered carefully. 'They're keeping her in overnight. Apparently she has a raised BP.'

'Oh dear . . .'

'Can I help?'

'I want the number of Jeff's garage. It's probably on the telephone pad. Heather thought they might service my car—but I've broken down and they'll have to tow it in, I'm afraid. Could you call them for me?'

'Sure. Where are you?'

Rachel repeated the instructions she had given the ambulance depot, ending, 'But I'm at the cottage just past there. I'm not sure anyone can get by until the car's moved.'

'You're not hurt, are you?'

She couldn't be sure whether there was amusement or concern in his voice.

'No, but I've an emergency on my hands at the cottage nearby. There's a woman in labour after falling and fracturing her leg. The ambulance should be here at any moment. I just hope they make it in time. Oh, must go,' she ended abruptly as Mrs McAllister gave a small scream. She was obviously having a stronger contraction this time.

It was probably one of the most fraught moments of Rachel's career, for her patient's moans persisted and, as she knelt beside her, Rachel's arms and hands were bruised and scratched as the nails bit into them. But this she barely felt as she wiped the beads of perspiration from the woman's forehead, her ears straining to hear the sound of the ambulance siren across the fields as it approached.

Oh, if only the midwife would return home and get her recorded message! How could this delay occur with the modern methods of contact in this day and age? It was ludicrous. Inside a hospital there had always been a way to alleviate unbearable pain, but not here on the floor of this kitchen-cum-living room of the small croft. Rachel could do little but be supportive until the ambulance arrived and just hope the baby held back long enough to receive medical help.

CHAPTER THREE

SLIDING a pillow under the fractured leg without disturbing it more than she must was torturous for Mrs McAllister, although, apart from her groans, she bore it stoically. Next, Rachel took a strong pillowcase and pinned it around both pillow and leg, and this acted as a gentle splint, curtailing movement and leaving just one leg to manipulate freely, which would still be difficult during the actual birth.

Between contractions Rachel scrubbed bowls with Savlon discovered beneath the kitchen sink, and upstairs took all the clean towels she could find, looking in vain for more suitable dressings and finding none, not even cotton wool. There were cot blankets, though, in a drawer, and baby nighties, obviously left over from the other children. These she brought down to air by the fire, together with a clean nightie for Mrs McAllister.

Next she stripped off her silk blouse and plaid skirt and tied another towel around her waist, immersing her hands and arms in more Savlon solution before kneeling again on the floor beside her patient, whose pains were stronger and coming thick and fast now.

Rachel was not at all happy about her condition. Quite apart from the leg fracture, she wondered how long the woman could hold out with pains like these tearing her apart. In a normal birth they would not be unduly severe—but this woman had suffered shock already. Oh why didn't the ambulance come? Or a neighbour, or someone to help?

The next pain left Mrs McAllister so exhausted that she seemed to fall into a semi-conscious state, and now

Rachel s brain cleared and the apprehension which had been building up disappeared. She was trained for something like this—and up to now she had done everything possible to prepare for the birth if it happened before medical help arrived. She *had* to cope.

She was just helping her patient through another pain when the door burst open and a red-faced Scotsman strode into the room, angrily slamming it behind him.

'I've just had to push a red car out of my way,' he began—then his face changed and he stood rooted to the spot at the sight of his wife among pillows on the floor; baby clothes by the fire; a half-undressed girl putting her finger to her lips as she got up and began to explain what had happened.

'I've called an ambulance but they must be delayed or can't find us. We need them, Mr McAllister. I am a nurse and that's my car out there. Could you phone the emergency services again, please? Oh, and then keep the children outside. This baby is coming soon . . .'

'My God,' he muttered, going to the phone, while his eyes never left his wife as she coped with yet another pain. Rachel murmured words of comfort and encouragement all through, until it subsided.

Soon he was able to tell her that they were coming out from Inverness. 'You were right, they couldn't find us. Did you tell them Little Braillay?'

'No, just Braillay . . .'

'They must have gone the other way then. She will be all right, won't she?'

Rachel could only smile at him gently. Not even he must know just how concerned she was becoming by the minute. Apart from murmuring, 'Greg . . .' and responding to his voice, Mrs McAllister had forgotten he was there, so he backed out of the door to the children, who were clamouring to come in, and talked firmly to them.

That was one problem alleviated, Rachel thought with some relief. Now for the next—she was about to have a premature delivery before the ambulance arrived; or could her patient hold out until then? She was fast losing strength, even though the baby's head was in the birth canal and moving downwards with every pain. There seemed no respite now for her. Rachel could see the dark hair, ready for precipitation, and oh —how she needed another pair or hands!

She didn't look round when the door opened and closed, but said quickly, 'Oh, Mr McAllister, I'm so glad you came back—I need you here . . .'

But it was Jonathan's voice against her ear murmuring, 'Then I made the right decision, my sweet . . .'

Rachel looked up for a brief second and as their eyes met a warm glow spread through her aching limbs. She could have wept with relief.

He was still wearing his shirt and jeans and was already rolling up his sleeves before plunging his hands into the sterile hot water in the bowl beside her.

'Be with you in a second,' he said. 'Just in time it seems. No ambulance?'

She shook her head, holding fast to her patient's hands while her moans grew deeper.

'I've brought one of Jeff's surgical bags,' Jonathan said in a low voice, then he too was kneeling on the floor holding Mrs McAllister's other leg while his eyes assessed the fracture and Rachel's efforts to hold it together. She saw his brow crease as again his eyes found hers and he realised the seriousness of the situation in which she had found herself.

After the next pain the woman looked up on hearing him.

'Hallo,' he said in his lovely deep voice, reassuring to any woman in travail. 'I'm Dr Paget. Try to relax. That's good. Breathe out if you can with this next pain . . .

We can see your baby, Mrs McAllister—it's got black hair, did you know? Right, here it comes . . .'

She had not strength to answer but he hadn't expected one as he steadied the leg on the pillow and watched Rachel's hands easing the baby's head through to rest in her hand while she swabbed the eyes clear of mucus.

All the time he spoke gently to the mother and she felt the strength of his hand instead of Rachel's—and then the baby was pushed out. Rachel waited to do the necessary things which, under these primitive conditions, were rather curtailed.

'You've got a little son,' Jonathan told her, but the poor woman was so exhausted she could barely manage a wan smile. 'Don't try to move. Nurse will tidy you up and then you can show him off to your family. I'll just take a look at him first.'

He shared Rachel's anxiety now as again their eyes met in understanding because the baby was reluctant to take his first breath; even when turned upside down and slapped he still showed no sign of life. Rachel tried to clear the air passage.

'I don't even have a sucker,' she breathed as the baby gave a kind of strangled gurgle.

'Give him to me.' Jonathan picked up the bag he had brought and went with the baby wrapped in a blanket across the room and out of Mrs McAllister's view.

'I'll manage,' he said grimly, 'but he's definitely premature, isn't he?'

Rachel hid her fears while she attended to his mother; then suddenly she heard the baby's first gasping breath, followed by a very weak wail of protest.

Slipping the clean nightie over the woman's head, she went to take the child from Jonathan and bring him to his mother, who was weeping tears of sheer exhaustion and was now trembling from shock reaction. Rachel dared not give her a warm drink because of the need for an anaesthetic when she reached hospital.

Any minute now the ambulance would be here. Meanwhile, Jonathan had broken the news to Mr McAllister and now he came into the room with the two small girls clinging one to each hand.

She and Jonathan saw him kneel down and leave a kiss in his wife's palm as he whispered huskily, 'Clever girl. We've got our son now. You just rest, my love.'

'The girls! Who's going to look after them if I'm in hospital, Greg?'

'I will—and I might go and fetch your mother presently. You're not to worry about a thing, darling. Just get to feel better, and you'll soon be back here with us . . .'

There was so much love between those two people there on the floor that Rachel felt a lump in her throat. It was quite beautiful—like a cameo; the two small girls were watching over the baby, not making any fuss, because they trusted in their family bond. As long as their father was around nothing could go wrong. Looking across the room Rachel saw that Jonathan was watching her face intently.

Just then the ambulance siren cut across the fields and within minutes it was at the gate and, to her intense relief, a nurse and doctor were there too, with all the modern equipment she had had to do without.

'It was fortunate you happened along,' the young doctor commented as he took in the situation with a swift glance around the room and asked Greg and the children to wait outside for a moment while the leg was encased in a plastic support and baby McAllister taken over by the nurse-in-charge. Jonathan went outside with them, leaving Rachel with a strange uncertainty lurking somewhere in the regions of her mind.

Greg decided to take the girls to his wife's mother

before following up the ambulance, and after it left Rachel asked if she might clear up before she left. And tidy herself too, for she realised that she was still in her slip.

'Ach, you know you can. Would you just leave the door key under the stone there if you want to be on your way? And thank you, Nurse. What would we have done without you? And you, Doctor, I'm very grateful,' he added as an afterthought.

'I'm just glad it went the way it did,' Jonathan told him. 'Your wife will be okay now, once she gets into hospital.'

When the cottage was empty, Jonathan came back to stand in the doorway, watching Rachel.

'Where do we start?' he asked, grimacing at the mess in the room.

'It won't take a minute. I know where everything goes but I'm afraid someone else will have to see about all this washing,' she assured him.

'I'll wait outside,' he muttered sheepishly.

At which she couldn't repress a smile as, man-like, he slid away from the mundane tasks and went to sit on the wooden seat. After a short while she was clean and dressed once more in her blouse and skirt; her hair was in place and the cottage was tidy—even the fire-guard checked and in place by the fire. Then, closing the door, she hid the key under the stone as requested and went out into the late afternoon sunshine.

Jonathan got up at once, disconcertingly near, and he waited for her to speak first. When she didn't because of the disturbing effect he was having on her senses, he said drily, 'Well, you don't have to say much. Just, "Thank you, Jonathan," would do very well.'

'Oh, you know how grateful I am,' she murmured. 'It was quite frightening for a time. The odds were against me.'

'Surely you knew that I would . . .?'

She shook her head. 'No, I didn't actually. Did you manage to phone the garage?'

'They're up the lane now. You don't have any idea what's wrong with your car?'

She shook her head. 'No, it just stopped dead.'

'Okay,' he said, holding open the small gate for her. 'I guess this isn't the time to remind you that you should have had it serviced, is it?'

He held open the door of his white car which was parked near the hedge and she felt all her normal resistance slipping away in the utter weariness of her limbs as she simply shook her head.

This prompted him to ask again, 'Are you sure you're not hurt, Rachel?'

'No, no, I'm fine. Just whacked.'

She waited to see her small red car being lifted on to the truck and then Jonathan drove her back to Inverness.

'I wonder if there is any more news of Heather,' she said thoughtfully as the buildings and hills of the town came into view. She soon realised that she must have driven around in a circle before lunch and hadn't been far from town at all.

'I shouldn't think so. I did think that she might be running a bit high before they left, although I said nothing to Jeff. After all, he should know.'

'Isn't that typical?' Rachel asked in a quiet voice. 'It's almost like having a plumber for one's husband, and a constantly dripping tap in the bathroom.'

'Or a doctor who doesn't recognise flu symptoms in his own family! But this one does notice when his girl is badly bruised—and are those scratch marks? Because, if so, they need something on them.'

'I'm not your girl, remember?' she reminded him, but glancing down at her wrists, swollen and red, rapidly changing colour all the time, wondered if he knew about her bruised arms too.

She shrugged, wincing as she eased her painful shoulder muscles. 'I'll be fine when I'm out of these clothes and into a hot bath.'

'Oh, I agree,' he chuckled, 'and you do smell as if you've just emerged from a maternity unit . . .'

They were turning into the road by the river now and, just as they used to before their break-up, they discussed the details in medical terms. Obviously, he had also shared her fears and the risks involved, as he commented, 'Of course, you couldn't splint the leg—not that it would have changed the pattern of the delivery.' He expelled his breath on a sigh. 'I just wish you had decided to spend the day with me instead. There were so many things we could have done—simply driven around the countryside or gone up into the hills . . .' He glanced at her thoughtful expression, caught sideways, and his dark eyes were smiling as he ventured, 'I suppose I should be grateful —we are at least talking to each other again, Rachel, and that's a start.'

She shook her head wearily. 'Oh, Jonathan,' she burst out, 'a start to what?'

'I'll show you, if you'll let me . . .' he murmured outrageously and, as the car turned into the driveway, his leg in denim jeans touched hers—whether accidentally or intentionally she didn't know or care. Her breath caught in her throat and, unfastening her seat-belt, she swung her legs on to the gravel. He had gained ground, already weakening her defences, and she was not going to be drawn again into the fascinating net he would weave. It was, she knew only too well, wonderful; with him she had known the pinnacle of happiness and ecstasy, a height to which only he had taken her. But it was too far to fall and had already caused irreparable damage. Much better to draw back now, before she couldn't help herself.

As she went towards the house the phone started to ring and, dashing into the hall, hoping that it wouldn't stop before she reached it, Rachel picked it up and heard Heather's voice.

'Were you out? I rang earlier . . .'

'I've just got back.'

'With Jonathan?'

'In a way—tell you when I see you. How are you?'

'Fine. I just want you to check my bag, the one behind my bedroom door, and get someone to drop it off, just in case I need it. Jeff is on theatre duty until late.'

'You haven't started, have you?' Rachel asked anxiously.

'No, but I might be here for a few days.' Heather sounded cheerful.

'I'll bring it myself. You *are* okay?'

'Nothing to worry about. Must go, love, there's a queue forming to use the phone. See you.'

'That was Heather,' she told Jonathan, hovering in the background.

'I'll take you in when you're ready.'

'Thanks,' Rachel said briefly.

'When were you thinking of driving back home, just supposing that your car is ready?'

'Friday at the latest. I'm on duty at eight on Monday morning. I just hope the damage isn't anything too drastic.'

'And if it is?'

'Then I'll go by train,' she said as she passed him, running lightly up the stairs, determined to give him no further inkling of the painful throbbing of her wrists and sore knees from kneeling beside Mrs McAllister.

She knew he hadn't moved but stood watching her, but she didn't look back and didn't see the look of defeat in his reflective eyes; nor would it have made any difference in her behaviour towards him if she had. Not then.

But she was very aware of him as she peeled off her clothes and knotted her housecoat, because she heard him go into his bedroom, at which she fled to the bathroom. Jonathan, smiling a little, heard the key turn in the lock.

Luxuriously, she let her body sink into the warm, scented water and felt it caressing her limbs. Even when the smarting pain started up again where nails had bitten into her flesh, she tried to ignore it. Not since her midwifery stint had she been quite so buffeted by a patient.

When she was ready to go back to her room, she wondered if Jonathan had gone downstairs yet. She didn't want to meet him on the landing. He might guess she had nothing on beneath the slinky pale green housecoat. So rather cautiously she unlocked the door and peered out.

He was leaning indolently against the door post of his room, his arms folded, his teasing manner having quite the opposite effect to the one he hoped for. She couldn't go back—that would be admitting defeat—so she glared at him disapprovingly while he, seeing the damp hair clinging in tiny tendrils around her elfin-shaped face, fresh and shiny and totally vulnerable, moved deliberately towards her across the carpet, unable to help himself.

His intention was obvious. She knew that look, but it was too late. One arm took her in a vice-like hold while the other lifted her chin, ignoring the twisting movement of her neck as he searched her eyes for something he hoped to find there, before homing down to her mouth, his lips yearning for hers, finding them warm and sweet as he remembered they were.

She moaned as she tried to escape them, which only incensed him even more, until he felt her cease to struggle, responding instead as her arm crept up of its own volition to the back of his head, just as she used to do; and she felt, once more, the familiar moulding of their limbs against each other. All her self-made resolutions dissolved as she clung to him, drowning beneath those passionate kisses, returning them now—kisses she had only ever experienced with Jonathan. Her hand slid over his muscled back under the silk shirt into which he had changed.

But when he slipped his hand inside her gown, his fingers on her skin, she somehow found strength to resist him, twisting away, to say breathlessly, 'Jonathan—no! That was unforgivable—you meant that to happen. Now let me go, please—I want to get dressed.'

He let her go at once, but she knew that he was disappointed, even angry, as she turned away from the still disturbing intentness of his gaze. His fingers gripped her wrist, turning her to face him again, causing her to wince. But he had forgotten her bruises now as he muttered, 'Don't do this to us, Rachel. We could have so much together.'

'What we *had*, Jonathan,' she reminded him. As his fingers tightened, she said fiercely, 'And you're hurting my wrist, damn you . . .'

Even now her breath came raggedly, her pulses still disturbingly uneven, but he let her hand go at once.

'I'm sorry, Rachel. I forgot your bruises. But so did you, a moment ago, I think . . .'

With that he turned and went down the stairs two at a time, and she heard the door slam as he went out to the garden. She saw him from her window, pacing around it, his hand in the pockets of beige pants which moulded his body so perfectly, and his eyes on the ground, while she recovered from the knowledge that he still had power over her senses, her body, and could apparently even undermine her reasoning.

How could she believe him, trust him again, she asked herself? He had never even attempted to offer any explanation about Cheryl's part in his life after their break-up. Nor, apparently, did he intend to do so. And Cheryl might even be coming back to England. How could she know that?

Surely he should expect her to have some pride? Or was he so full of his own sense of power over her, so innately selfish, that he could choose to ignore everyone else's desires but his own?

'Rachel Woods—you're a fool!' she whispered to her face in the mirror as she brushed her hair as hard as she could bear, then coaxed it into shape. 'You're still in love with him—you know that, don't you? And *he* knows it!'

Somehow she had to get this thing into perspective. The best thing would be to leave now—not see the week through. Or perhaps he would decide to go soon. Yet Rachel knew that she didn't want that. Being near him again was like falling in love for the first time. She wanted to keep seeing him, to talk to him, to feel the glow and warmth of love's awakening all over again. She had to admit that. Because he had just proved something to both of them, hadn't he? But then she didn't trust or believe in him any more. He might leave her again, when the next girl came along, and next time might be even more shattering. No, she couldn't risk that . . .

Reason decreed that she should never let any man do that to her again. Only—how could one be sure?

Jonathan also seemed to have reached a decision, and instead of the constraint between them she had been expecting, even bolstering herself up for, he was in his most co-operative mood, with a return of the slightly arrogant bearing he wore with his white professional coat. And she knew that approach. While thoughtful and quite caring to some patients, he could be sharp and straight to the point with others who wasted his time or made nuisances of themselves or disregarded his advice or instructions; the same with the nursing staff too. Yet today he had been wonderful with Mrs McAllister and the Scots family in the tiny cottage, Rachel mused as she started on the evening meal.

He was behaving as if nothing unusual had happened upstairs, coming through into the kitchen where Rachel was preparing a salad, and asking what time she would like to go to the hospital.

'Before or after supper?'

'We could eat now if you like, then go in. Visiting hours are from seven till eight.'

'Right. Can I help here?'

'Yes, you could slice off some of the chicken if you like. Heather did plan this for tonight but I don't know what time Jeff will be back. There are jacket potatoes so I hope that's all right with you. Oh, and baked apples.'

'Nice and homely,' he grinned. 'You should marry a farmer—or maybe a doctor?'

'I'm not sure I want to marry anyone just yet,' she retorted, but he had turned his back so that she couldn't see his face. She did have a suspicion that he was amused about something—though, for the life of her, she couldn't think what. She intended now to play it her way—much less complicated than the raw, unleashed emotions which had been let loose between them earlier this evening. Maybe if they kept it on a nice, civilised basis . . .? But she had to admit that it *was* rather wonderful, having him around, just the same—if a trifle disconcerting.

It was a strange feeling later to walk through the hospital corridor beside Jonathan, both wearing casual clothes instead of the starched caps and aprons and white coats of Great Cedars, sticklers for tradition and protocol.

The atmosphere was no different, though perhaps a little more casual; one tended to talk in whispers in the Cedars' corridors and wards. The familiar smell of antiseptic greeted them the moment the swing doors closed behind them on the maternity floors, and they found Heather sitting up in bed and very obviously bored.

'Oh, thanks for coming,' she said gratefully. 'What I am doing here in this bed I can't think! It's ridiculous! I'm supposed to be a bit toxic, of all things . . .'

'Oh, come on,' Jonathan broke in, 'who's kidding who? If your BP is up, of course they have to monitor you for a day or two—and you know that as well as anyone.'

'Yes, well, *why* is it? Up, I mean?'

'Perhaps you've been doing too much,' Rachel suggested.

'Hey, you aren't talking to a novice exactly! I know all the answers, which is why I'm so frustrated. I felt fine before . . . Besides, you're going to have to cope at home,' she finished anxiously.

'That's the last thing you have to worry about,' Rachel reassured her. 'And it is only until Friday. I'll be taking off then . . .'

'And I think very probably that I shall as well,' Jonathan broke in.

Both girls looked at him questioningly.

'For two reasons, actually,' he said easily. 'One, I have an appointment early next week at a hospital in Gloucester and two, I rather think Rachel might be coming back with me in my car. She broke down and there's no way they're going to get hers back on the road in time.'

'How do you know?' Rachel flared suddenly.

'When you were in the bath there was a phone call,' he said unconcernedly. 'It wasn't good news, the mechanic at the garage informed me—but if you ring back after eight they will put you in the picture. You have to make a decision of sorts, it seems.'

'You should have told me,' she said crossly.

'I think something else came up which completely obliterated it from my mind,' he said mischieviously, watching the blush slowly suffuse her face.

'I see we're back to normal,' Heather commented, 'and it was really nice to see you both come through that door together and actually compatible for once. So —I'm to lose you both?'

'You don't really need guests at the moment, love. Just look after yourself,' Rachel said gently.

'Well, if being here has achieved some harmony, it was well worth it,' Heather insisted. 'You're like you used to be together.'

'Not quite,' Jonathan grinned broadly, 'but we're working on it.' His tigerish eyes were turned fully on Rachel now, and looking away she saw that the nurse and a man passing the door reminded her of Greg McAllister. Of course, it *was* him. She jumped up and hurried after him. The nurse was taking him to see his son, be it only through the glass window of the nursery.

Mr McAllister was delighted to see her, explaining that she had been with his wife that morning, to the nurse in blue by his side.

'The baby is doing fine now,' the staff nurse reported, giving Rachel a knowing look. But Rachel could see that, in spite of the various wires, Baby McAllister looked as if he was going to make it.

'He's certainly got a little more colour,' she commented. 'And your wife? Is she here on this floor?'

'Mrs McAllister has just gone down to theatre,' staff nurse said. 'Fragmented fracture of the tibia. They're going to reduce it. It must have been a nasty experience for both of you.'

'I'm a little out of practice,' Rachel said wryly. 'How is she now?'

'Surprisingly well—she's a very brave lady, your wife, Mr McAllister.'

'You don't need to tell me that, Nurse,' he said quietly. 'I just hope she comes out of this all right.'

'Go home and don't worry. I'll ask Night Sister to give you a call later, if you like.'

Back in Heather's room Rachel reported her news, Jonathan having recounted the events of Rachel's day to Heather's listening ears, but leaving out the traumatic birth details.

When Rachel said that Mrs McAllister had gone to theatre they all realised that very probably Jeff would be operating.

'He'll probably be late tonight,' Heather warned. 'He said he had another fracture and also an emergency coming in. But we shall be able to keep you posted about Mrs McAllister if you're interested.'

'Of course I am,' Rachel protested. 'He's my baby!'

'And mine,' Jonathan reminded her, but this time she refused to let herself be drawn into those depths of tawny speculation—while he waited to see the effect they would arouse in her own cool dark brown eyes. Mirrors of the soul was very apt with regard to her. She simply could not mask her true feelings because her eyes always gave her away.

Rachel got up from her chair and said goodbye to Heather, promising to come again the following day, '. . . if you have to stay here. Meanwhile, everything at home is fine. I'll feed the brutes! Must go, I've got to find out the worst about my car . . .'

In the words of the mechanic at Jeff's garage, the car could have fallen apart at any time, and Rachel was very fortunate to get away with a straight breakdown.

'It's worthless with all that rust under its bonnet,' he ended. 'We could only take it off you for scrap.'

There was no way she could dispute that and Jonathan even offered to accompany her next day to the garage —to see for herself and perhaps get further advice.

At the end of it all Rachel simply walked away from her little red car, sadly but wiser.

Which was why, on Friday morning, very early, she and Jonathan set off for Gretna Green, where they would be staying at the hotel there for the night.

CHAPTER FOUR

Loch Ness was shrouded in mist, ethereal spirals rising upwards in moving patterns as Jonathan and she drove along the shore road.

Rachel said, disappointment husking her voice, 'I did so want you to see it as it was when I came here last week. There's nothing to see today . . .'

'On the contrary,' Jonathan said thoughtfully, 'I think it is the real atmosphere of this somewhat sombre lake. There are a lot of other lakes to see on the way down. I thought we might make Loch Lomond for lunch. Jeff told me the name of a good place for food with a view of the water. Okay with you?'

'Fine,' she told him, a little smile playing around her mouth. Everything was fine as long as they were together this way. She had very slowly and tentatively begun to trust him again, partly because of his charm and careful approach over the past day or two, but mainly because of the shared trauma at the cottage. There had been a return to the same level of medical urgency which they both understood and responded to without question.

He leaned forward and took his map from the shelf, putting it on her knees, and Rachel saw his mouth twitch at the corners when he threw her a quizzical glance.

'I've marked the route I intend taking, Rachel. You're going to navigate, but I don't want to find that we're miles out of our way, or half-way up a mountain,' he ended with a wide grin, which she didn't find amusing.

She told him indignantly, 'I drove up to Inverness, you know—*and* navigated myself.'

She heard his indrawn breath as he gave her a swiftly sceptical glance. 'It was a miracle you arrived at all,' he said drily.

'Ah, but I did, Jonathan,' she murmured, her head bent low over the map as she studied his markings. So she didn't see an expression which was somewhat different cross his face, serious now and concentrated, his eyes watching the road ahead.

'Fort William ahead.' Rachel broke the silence after a time. 'I stopped at a café here. The coffee is very good,' she added hopefully.

'Okay. Where is it?'

'About a mile further on. Just on the left. Look, there's snow on Ben Nevis! Quite a lot for early autumn, wouldn't you think?'

He didn't answer, simply nodded, until they were parked; then, unlocking his seat-belt he got out, stretching his muscles, his lithe body taut beneath the rust sweater and brown tailored corded pants.

'What a setting . . .' he said, expelling his breath on a contented sigh when Rachel joined him, and casually slipping his arm around her shoulders as they stood together looking up at the mountain. If he felt her tremble at his touch he gave no sign, as he asked, 'Do you think it is warm enough to stay outside?' Only then did he look down into her upturned face.

'Why not?' Her voice trembled too. She heard it and wondered if he had. She hoped not. The last thing she wanted was him to suspect that once again he was evoking a physical reaction to his touch, his male nearness, as always before.

Ben Nevis towered fearsomely above them, the snow sparkling like diamonds on its cragged peaks as the morning sunshine broke through the clouds. Jonathan kept his arm possessively around Rachel as they walked over to one of the white-painted wrought-iron tables and didn't let her go until they sat facing each other.

She watched his face in profile, the muscles in his chin as he nonchalantly crossed one leg over the other knee while he surveyed the outlying foothills.

'You know,' he said reflectively, 'this reminds me very much of Canada. Of the weekend I spent at Banff in Alberta. The spruce trees grow all up the mountains there too. Actually, we had a trailer hooked up right in the foothills in a forest of larch pines. Rachel, you have no idea of the scent of those pines—until we barbecued the T-bone steaks and the wood-smoke took over! There was a pile of pine logs all sawn ready for us when we arrived and a kind of stove with a grid on the top. It was sacrilege really, introducing the smell of scorched beef into such an idyllic place. I guess it was one of those weekends one remembers afterwards with nostalgia.'

Until then, Rachel had been with him, sharing the scene he had drawn in her imagination. But now a sharp pang shot through her chest and she couldn't bear it.

'Were you there with Dr Summers?' She hadn't meant to ask so blatantly, so obviously, and the words came out too quickly. But she had to know.

Jonathan looked at her in genuine surprise, his brows coming together in a frown. 'Good heavens, no. Why should she be?'

'I thought . . .' Rachel began lamely.

'There were three of us. Myself and two other guys, one of whom was the paediatric specialist researching the collagen-type diseases too. It was largely due to him that I got through so much work in my year there. He was extremely helpful. I owe him a lot. The other guy, also at the hospital, shared his apartment with me.'

He paused while their coffee was put on the table, still frowning a little, while the impact of her question slowly registered.

His chin came up when he asked tersely, 'Why did you imagine that Cheryl was there with me? Why, Rachel?' he demanded impatiently. She knew that he was angry now. 'Good God, that's been it all along, hasn't it? You really thought we had something going, didn't you? Because we saw a lot of each other, which was to be expected under the circumstances, seeing that she was working with me, and we are both doctors. Then the research grant council decided I should go, for a year at least, which you knew about. And because it seemed consistent, we flew out on the same plane direct. I'm afraid, my sweet, you surmised the rest, which was a pity.'

When she didn't comment, he went on, 'You see, Rachel, I thought you were rather taking things for granted—resenting that year apart. You certainly behaved that way, deliberately cooling off. But I thought that before I left there would be time to talk about it—only you took off to Wales, didn't you? Still without telling me why. I called you on that last day and your mother said you were refusing to come to the phone. What else was I to think? I had a great many other decisions to work out regarding my own future. I was hurt—I'll admit that—but my ego has a way of recovering. And then I saw you again, only to discover that I had been branded something of a philanderer. Is that right?'

He saw by her face that it was and pursued the matter still further while she fervently wished that he would leave it alone and reached nervously for her coffee.

'What I don't understand, Rachel, is why?' he asked sternly. 'You're not a small-minded girl. Unless your rigid ideas of black or white and no in-betweens blurred your discretionary powers.'

'Don't!' Her eyes wavered under his scrutiny. 'You

did nothing about it, Jonathan. I made myself believe it was what you wanted. Besides . . .'

'Besides what?'

'Dr Summers also gave me the impression that you had something going between you, so . . .'

'You just opted out,' he snapped.

'Yes.'

'The easy way.'

'Is that what you think?' Her voice trembled as she played with her spoon. His hand came to grasp hers firmly. She raised her eyes to his then, liquid pools of blackness in her pale face as they encountered his, gravely searching for what he needed to know.

'So I was relegated to the past—is that it?' She nodded. 'And am I still there, Rachel?'

'Not quite,' she said tremulously. 'I'm working on it.'

He withdrew his hand and lifted his cup unsmilingly. 'Then don't take too long, honey,' he said, deliberately flippant. 'But before we leave, Dr Summers . . .'

'Yes?' Rachel asked too quickly.

'She got herself engaged to the senior house surgeon at the hospital as soon as we arrived in Canada. It was already on the cards before she came over here.'

He stood up, waiting for her to join him. 'Time to move on, don't you think?' he asked gently.

Walking beside him to the car without speaking, Rachel felt rather foolish. Also, there was a bereft feeling somewhere inside her mind. Probably because the righteous smugness she had built around her thoughts of Jonathan had gone. She had been at fault too, and her impulsive flight to Wales hadn't been a very good decision either. If she had stayed and tried to see it logically, she would certainly not have endured such a miserably fraught year. She had been jealous of his time away from her; while to Jonathan it was a big step towards his future recognition in the field he had chosen one day to specialise in. Any private liaisons, however promising, must take second place for the time being.

He was quite aware of her thoughts now as she sat beside him, lips pursed, gazing in front of her, but he wasn't going to admit to it, as he drove in almost continual silence, apart from asking and getting directive instructions from time to time.

Then, as they came to Glen Coe and the mountains towered high on either side of the pass, both were so enthralled at the grandeur and cruel beauty of those awesome peaks that they couldn't escape from saying so, words breaking through the silence.

'I'm sure this place hasn't changed since that picture in my old history book at school,' Rachel said, gazing up at the hills where the historic massacre of the Macdonalds and Campbells happened. 'That was in 1692—I think.'

'I'm sure you're right,' Jonathan murmured, throwing her an amused glance. 'Do you want to stop or shall we push on? I've no inclination to climb up there. I see there are a few climbers—but it looks very treacherous to me. And there goes the mountain rescue team. So someone is obviously in distress. They're very well equipped, apparently. Hazardous job that . . .'

The rescue team disappeared between the mountains and Rachel suggested they move on. The car shot forward, following the winding road over the hills and into the valleys, through fantastic scenery and eventually along the banks of Loch Lomond. It was a simple matter to find Jeff's eating place. But as they gazed out over the lake, sun-dappled yet misty too, Rachel was conscious of a disconcerting feeling of insecurity once more where Jonathan was concerned.

If only she really knew how much he cared—or

wanted to care. As if guessing her thoughts, his hand moved to cover hers in her lap, forcing her fingers apart, moving his own gently between them.

'There is no need for that serious face, my sweet,' he murmured close to her ear. 'I thought you would enjoy today. It's the first time we've been alone, and now that we have cleared the air, as it were, can't we relax and appreciate it? You're all tied up in knots still, aren't you? Have another glass of wine.'

'Oh, no thanks. I'm not tense in the least. But I was thinking rather hard,' she admitted. 'You see, I thought —oh, it doesn't matter now. I was wrong. I'm sorry.'

'Don't be. We still have tonight and most of tomorrow. Let's make the most of it,' he finished, his low voice thrilling her through, as always, while she hastily retreated to the powder room before he realised the effect he was having. It was deliberately instigated, she knew, which was why she fought against it. Just how much did she mean to him? If only she knew beyond any doubt. But Jonathan had no intention of committing himself further. Not then.

They continued on the more mundane journey to the Forth Bridge and through Glasgow where the traffic problems took every ounce of Jonathan's concentration, then to Hamilton where they stopped briefly before continuing on down towards the border.

And now Gretna was signposted. 'Eleven miles.' Rachel stretched her body, cat-like, and Jonathan, quick to be aware of her more relaxed state, reached to touch her wrist, immediately aware of her quickening pulse.

He grinned at her as he said teasingly, 'I hope you haven't any ideas about getting me hooked over the anvil. The forge is still there, I believe.'

'Yes, it is. But no marriages have been performed there for ages. Besides, it wouldn't be legal.'

'Who cares about that in these enlightened days? Marriage seems to be on the decline anyway.'

'Don't you believe that!' she said hotly. 'More and more people want to get married.'

'But not until they've been together for quite a while first.'

'So—what's wrong with that? As long as one is sure that . . .'

'Exactly. But I don't think that's possible. To be that sure, I mean. People change. I've seen it so often.'

She had no answer to that, but a cloud seemed to have obscured the sun a little.

He turned into a lane with the signpost directing them to the village of Gretna, a half-mile distant. Ahead were the whitewashed cottages of the small community and there, among the trees at the end of a drive-in, the famous Gretna Hall Hotel where they were spending that night.

Jonathan had telephoned the evening before to check their bookings and now he seemed to take over, to Rachel's secret amusement, especially when she realised that their rooms were next to each other on the first floor. Neither spoke as they went up the carpeted stone staircase, still part of the original building, the blackened beams bearing out the authenticity of that, as did the heavy doors and iron locks still in use.

Jonathan waited while she fitted her key into her door.

'Yours is along there,' she observed, tongue in cheek.

'I know. I was curious to see if there is a communicating door,' he said wickedly, which she chose to ignore, relieved to see there was not. It was a nice room; the windows overlooked the parkland and each had a wide window seat.

'Romantic,' he said softly, resting his hands on her shoulders. 'And there are two beds . . .'

She looked away hastily from the questing look in his lazy eyes and put her head against his chest for a second before gently pushing him out into the corridor.

'Dinner is at seven,' she said, her eyes laughingly discounting his disappointed expression. 'I want to freshen up now.'

'Okay,' he said philosophically, 'but drinks first in the bar. We're going to make the most of tonight, my sweet.'

There was no mistaking the inference he intended her to make and her heartbeats quickened as she closed the door after him. She was very aware now of her reactions to being with Jonathan again. Her heart felt light and the sparkle had returned to the dark brown eyes gazing back at her in the mirror as she brushed her hair up from the nape of her neck. They were still glowingly speculative as she applied lipstick and make-up, feeling an instinctive urge to be different tonight.

The dress lying on the bed was as yet unworn, a holiday extravagance which Heather had insisted was a perfect foil for her brown eyes when they had seen it in a boutique in the main street at Inverness. Now Rachel had to admit that the deep shade of violet really did something for her as she fastened the neck. The peplum waist hugged her softly. Long sleeves, gathered into wristbands, and the high neck, gave her a new elegance. She had brushed her hair softly across her forehead, the feminine instinct to please and captivate the man she was dining with assertive in her mind.

A decisive knock on her door startled her into looking at her watch. Was she late for dinner? But no, it was still early.

Jonathan was impatient. He came into the room wearing his dark suit, looking every inch the consultant he hoped one day to become and taking in every detail of her appearance.

'You look marvellous!' His eyes reflected more than his words and she lifted her face to feel his searching mouth on hers.

They were both breathing deeply when he let her go, standing back to look more fully this time. 'I like it,' he said appreciately as he held the door open for her and they went down the wide stairs together; the evening ahead was full of promise.

A log fire burned in the lounge bar. They sat watching the glowing red embers as they sipped dry Martinis, looking at the various relics on the walls, both receptive to the relaxed atmosphere of the hotel.

Later, when Jonathan leaned across to refill her wine glass during the main course, Rachel confided to him with sparkling eyes and a new lightness in her voice, 'I am so enjoying this meal. I expect it's because I had nothing to do with its preparation, don't you?'

'Oh, definitely.' He smiled indulgently, but then something deeper crept into his expression. His eyes became disconcertingly intent and she felt the hot colour suffuse her face before he resumed his eating. He knew now, without a doubt, that he could still evoke her deepest responses simply by one concentrated look.

When the sweet trolley arrived they were talking in hospital jargon. She wasn't sure how they had slipped into it but it was never far from his mind anyway. Now they were truly on the same wavelength because she loved it when he opened up to her in this way, enthusing on a new and exciting advance in medical science and paediatric nursing. Then, quite abruptly, he stopped in mid-sentence, smiling ruefully as he stirred his black coffee.

'This is unforgivable, Rachel. Sorry . . . In a few days we shall be involved in our different ways with this very thing. But not tonight,' he ended on a firm note.

She sighed deliciously, glowing in his masterly

approach which she suspected was romantically motivated, deliberately or not. She had been starved for so long that it was easy to accept and bask in this kind of warmth. Even so, she was fully aware of his careful but positive course. He was hoping tonight would become one of rediscovery for them both—and it was what she wanted too, desperately. He knew that already. But . . .

Strains of Scottish music reached them from the ballroom and they wandered in to stand on the edge of the floor watching the dancers. The band were in traditional dress and one of them played nostalgically haunting music on the bagpipes while another sang Gaelic songs.

Then suddenly all this changed and an air of gaiety crept in. On impulse Jonathan swept her into his arms and she was spinning around the floor with him, regardless of the authenticity of the steps to which they were neither of them accustomed. But it was fun and as much as Rachel could do to keep up with him. All around them kilts were swinging and burly Scotsmen danced lightly in size ten shoes, just for the sheer enjoyment of it.

After that the evening became simple escapism. Jonathan's touch was electric, his eyes full of promise and now her confidence was restored, back to the early days. She was excitingly in love all over again. Breathlessly, deliriously happy because this was Jonathan as she had seldom seen him and the past was now obliterated in a new togetherness, marvellously away from everyone who knew them. Tomorrow, when they must return to other environments, simply had no part in today.

As if guessing her thoughts, Jonathan said huskily against her ear, 'This is something I didn't expect—an added bonus. And we still have tonight, my sweet.' Then, taking her hand, he led her off the floor and along to the bar, quietly ordering two brandies.

'Oh, I don't drink brandy,' she protested.

'Make an exception,' he told her softly, taking her to sit in the corner seat beside the smouldering embers of the log fire again. From the ballroom the music still drifted through to them and now she was intimately aware of Jonathan in a way she had forgotten she could be. So when his eyes held a silent question, Rachel went with him into the reception hall and across to the stairs, deliciously languorous as they climbed them together, his arm around her possessively now.

The rosy glow of the lamp beside her bed contributed its part in creating just the right atmosphere and as she went to draw the rose velvet curtains across the windows, kneeling on the window seat to reach them, she felt his arms around her, his sensitive hands on her breasts, gentle, yet just as she had remembered them so many achingly lonely times.

'Oh, Rachel . . .' he groaned, and now her limbs dissolved as she felt him move even closer and she turned into his arms.

His voice was husky with passion now. 'I want you,' he murmured against her lips.

'I—I want you too . . .' This, then, was to be her ultimate surrender.

Her dress lay in a pool on the floor. His touch on her body was all delight and exquisite recapture, her senses responding as he had known they would, once he had broken through the self-imposed defences she had put between them.

'I love you so!' The words burst from her lips and she waited desperately for him to say that he loved her too.

'I want you,' he muttered against her skin, 'isn't that enough, Rachel? You have to be aware how much I want to make love to you.'

'No, oh—no . . .!' It came from her heart—a cry of bitter disappointment because he had so deliberately avoided saying the words she longed to hear. She felt the tears wet on her flushed face before he realised that her hands were attempting to push him away from her.

'Why? You want me too—you know that you do,' he muttered hoarsely. 'So why are you crying?'

She could only turn her face into the pillow while tears of frustration and poignant misery flowed unchecked.

He was angry and puzzled by her rejection of him now. 'Why?' he asked again harshly.

'I really love you . . .' she said brokenly. 'But I don't think you love me—not in the same way. It's as simple as that. So I don't want to go any further. Please, Jonathan, try to understand. Just go away!'

He swung his legs to the floor and she knew he was attempting to control his disappointment.

'I don't, I'm afraid,' he told her curtly.

'I know. Don't you see? That's why! I love you, Jonathan. It could have been so perfect tonight . . .' Her voice trembled. 'But you only want me physically, and it isn't enough.'

'That's ridiculous,' he said shortly as he started to dress. 'You aren't a child, Rachel. You knew where we were heading all evening.'

'Yes,' she said sadly. 'I really felt that we were back together again. It was a lovely evening; the whole day was, in fact . . .'

He was silent for a moment, then shrugged, turning to look at her; the sheet was pulled up to her chin as she gazed back at him and her brown eyes were luminous with repressed emotion.

'I had hoped,' he said, unsmiling, 'that you had become a little more mature in the year we've been apart, Rachel. You certainly gave that impression at Jeff's. I guess I expected you to be the way you were—the image of you in your uniform, whether you were wearing it or not, I suppose. Instead, you had emerged from the chrysalis into a sophisticated woman. I was shattered. I realised how much I had missed you. Okay, I still feel the same way. But it isn't enough for you, obviously.'

When she didn't reply he went on more gently. 'Look, there is no other woman I want to be with as much as you, honey. But I can't and won't commit myself. Not yet, anyway, to anything more permanent. Neither should you. The last thing I need is an all-enveloping emotional entanglement cluttering up my life. I've got to be free to see where I'm going first. Can't you understand that?'

He put one finger under her chin and leaned to kiss her lightly. 'You know how I feel about you, Rachel. It will have to do for now. Get some sleep. We should make an early start in the morning so I suggest breakfast at eight. Good night.'

He didn't look back, closing the door quietly behind him.

She got up, pulling on her dressing-gown, and went to draw back the curtains, looking out on to the avenue of trees, the leaves golden in the floodlamps concealed among their branches. Perhaps there might never be another more romantically motivated evening than tonight, she mused. Why must she spoil it all by her need to be sure of his love? Was love to him simply a physical thing? If that were so, then it definitely wasn't what she wanted and needed from the man who held her heart as well as her body. There was no stability in Jonathan's kind of relationship and she couldn't go along with it. It hurt that he was adamant about it, even at the risk of losing her. Which gave her a little comfort, because she had somehow managed to say no even while she wondered sadly where they would go from there.

She was dressed early and went down before eight,

stopping by the reception desk to settle her bill, which she had insisted on doing separately.

Behind her, someone came up the steps and into the hall. She didn't look round until Jonathan said quietly, 'Good morning—you're up early.'

'So are you.' And turning, she saw that he was regarding her with a tolerant smile as one might a naughty child after a tantrum.

'I've found my way around the village and chatted up a donkey bemoaning his lot in a field. Nice, understanding creatures, donkeys—very attentive listeners.'

She couldn't restrain a smile then and they both went to collect a morning paper from the centre table before going through to the dining-room together. This morning Jonathan wore his Dr Paget image. Last night he was the lover, the pursuer; but today he was a little remote from her, and if they had been on the wards or in the clinic it would have been a morning to make no slip-ups and avoid any form of irritation, or beware.

Suddenly she was homesick for the wards at the Cedars. She wanted to be back there again as part of its hum—the heartbeat of the busy hospital. She wanted to be doing again. Well, on Monday she would be once more donning her print dress and white cap, tying her plastic apron around her waist and delving into a round of injections, bandages, bedpans, lifting cumbersome patients, checking and measuring saline drips and every other kind of duty. Washing, feeding, changing night-dresses and bed sheets, remembering names and keeping report sheets all needed to be done. She'd be aching at the end of the day in every muscle in her body. And, somehow, always coming up with a smile. Because patients expected that.

Rachel was made aware suddenly of a waitress patiently standing at her side.

'Oh, just grapefruit and toast, please,' she managed

to say, because Jonathan was eyeing her quizzically across the table.

'Where were you, Rachel? Back into yesterday?'

'No. Actually, I was thinking about the hospital. I shall be quite glad to get back.'

'Really? Well, we do have a long drive ahead of us. Are your parents expecting you today?'

She smiled mischievously. 'Yes, but not you. They don't know about my car yet.'

After breakfast there was just time to have a quick look inside the renowned blacksmith's shop and view the famous forge, the anvil over which so many marriages were performed—all those young lovers who came here to get wed. Rachel found it so romantic. Her face softened as she thought about it. But Jonathan was more forthright.

'I think marriage as such is outmoded and quite unnecessary,' he commented drily. 'Unless one intends to start children, of course. And that's something no one in his right mind would undertake lightly. I have my own views on that. So, apparently, have you.'

'I think that marriage is right when two people love each other and want to be together for the rest of their lives,' Rachel said thoughtfully.

'Now how can two people possibly be that sure?' he argued impatiently.

As there was no answer to that they both decided to change the subject, and neither of them spoke again until they were driving down the M4 motorway and about to pull in for a pub lunch at the next exit.

Tentatively she broached the subject of his own future.

'You've got another iron in the fire, I presume. Not necessarily coming back to Great Cedars, but . . .'

'But I might. It's quite possible. It depends where I can work with my research coming into focus. I want to get to work on Schonlein's Syndrome and other inflammatory diseases as soon as possible.'

Rachel was enthusiastic. She had been reading up the new nursing methods coming into the wards quite recently. And somewhere along the way they had slipped back into a less volatile way of conversing. Each was stimulating the conversation as they usually did as the miles sped by and at last Bristol and Bath were signposted.

Rachel said quietly, 'You know, I should be quite happy if you dropped me at Bristol, Jonathan. I can get a train from there. That is if you want to be with your parents sometime today. Because it's too far to drive back tonight.'

He shrugged. 'I haven't given it much thought. Shall we wait and see what evolves? I'm driving you right home.'

'My mother will insist that you stay tonight.'

'I'm hoping so,' he responded audaciously, his hand sliding towards hers on the seat.

His touch sent responses shooting through her body immediately, so that involuntarily her fingers curled around his.

He shook his head disbelievingly. 'I have to be quite mad to let you disrupt my life this way,' he said positively. 'Where do we go from here?'

'I think,' she said solemnly, 'that question must be left in abeyance for the moment. Right now, we're about to cross the Severn Bridge. I'll get the toll tickets on this side, shall I?'

Fifteen minutes later they were in Wales and heading for home.

Rachel wasn't goint to admit to the intensely happy feeling which had started some miles back as she sat with her shoulder touching his. The cracks had been cemented over. They hadn't lost for ever that special fusion of feeling which bound them together She kept her thoughts to herself, hidden, but so did Jonathan, his face impassive as he drove alongside a phone box and watched her get out to tell her parents of their impending arrival.

'Mummy?'

'Rachel! Where are you?'

'Two hours away. But I'm not alone. It's a long story. Jonathan was staying in Scotland too and he has driven me down. My car is off the road, I'm afraid.'

'You're all right?'

'I'm fine. See you soon.'

If her parents were thrown a little by the news that Jonathan was coming too, when they thought he was still in Canada and certainly not on very close terms with Rachel after the trauma of his departure, they behaved impeccably. When the car drew up in front of their stone farmhouse in the hills, surrounded by green fields and grazing sheep and a quiet peacefulness which was refreshingly welcome after the noise and fast-moving traffic of the motorways, they were both waiting at the gate. They both saw Jonathan lean across and kiss Rachel's mouth the moment the car stopped and her quick blush as she fumbled with the door catch.

'I suppose they haven't gone and got themselves married,' her father said slowly.

'Of course not. Nothing like that,' his wife said positively, flashing him a reproving glance which he ignored.

'I don't know, they do have that kind of look about them . . .' David Woods observed thoughtfully, as Rachel came towards them followed by the tanned and self-assured Dr Jonathan Paget, carrying her suitcases.

CHAPTER FIVE

REBECCA Woods couldn't have loved her only daughter more, but she found it difficult and unnecessary to show her feelings and there were no questions; well, not obvious ones, and not straight away.

Rachel's father was a typical Welsh hill farmer, a very down-to-earth man whose living depended on his sheep and a few head of beef cattle.

Jonathan admired them both very much and chatted easily over a delicious meal of roast lamb flavoured with rosemary and brandied raspberries and cream to follow. Everyone was feeling replete as they sat around a log fire in the sitting-room with their coffee later.

Now Rachel told them a few of the happenings at Inverness and how Jonathan came to be there. He filled in with the garage report on her car and why he had driven her home.

'And where did you stay last night? Gretna, was it?' Rebecca asked innocently.

'Yes,' Rachel put in, hastening to describe the Scottish entertainment laid on for them and how much Jonathan enjoyed the setting of the renowned Gretna Green. 'He even went for a walk before breakfast.'

'So you'll be going back to Cedars, I dare say . . .?'

'I'm not sure yet, Mrs Woods. I have one or two options still open, but I hope so.'

'I have to be back on Sunday night,' Rachel put in. 'Which means going by train. I think there is one around four-thirty, isn't there?' she questioned, looking across at her father, who nodded.

'If it's still running . . .'

'And I must be off first thing in the morning,' Jonathan told them. 'Perhaps I could phone my parents later and put them in the picture. They are used to me just turning up, but they must be half expecting me.'

'Why not do it now?' David interposed.

'And we'll get on with the dishes.' Rebecca rose, followed by Rachel and, from the kitchen, they heard him talking on the phone in the hall.

Quite soon afterwards, Rachel went off to her bedroom. She had a desperate need to be alone. It was too much just to sit opposite Jonathan, making small talk when he obviously had no intention of enlightening any of them about his future plans. Besides which, she had to deliberately avoid his tigerish eyes, speculatively teasing and, in some way, overpowering tonight. He was, she knew, reminding her of last night, or what might have been, and she was feeling just a little angry with him. He really thought she was regretting her refusal to go on—but he was wrong. She knew now that she had been right. She needed far more from her lover than he was prepared to give. She wanted true involvement, not just a *divertissement*.

When she had said good night just now, his eyebrows had lifted as if he was surprised, or amused—she couldn't be sure which, and her senses were still confused.

Opening the dormer window under the eaves, she leaned out to take deep breaths of cool night air. Outside, the hills were steeped in darkness now, and only the lights of the small town in the valley were visible. There were stars though, scattered across the blue-black sky, just as she remembered from childhood. The silence too—it was something one listened to here in the hills. It brought a calm to her jumbled thoughts and ease to her restless body.

It was some time before she heard her parents come up and saw Jonathan's light go on to reflect in the darkness outside, and she wondered what he and they had been discussing for so long. She was suddenly too tired to care any more.

Next morning, after an early breakfast, he was ready to leave. Rachel and her mother stood at the gate as he got into his car and threw them both a quick smile, before starting up the engine. Then, with a wave of his hand, he was gone.

'So that's that,' her mother said, looking a little lost. 'One never knows quite where one is with Jonathan, does one?'

'I know what you mean,' Rachel said briefly, as she watched the roof of his car between the hedgerows, negotiating the narrow, winding lanes until it reached the main road.

He hadn't said when they would see each other again, just given her shoulder a squeeze as he was leaving—not even a kiss. Almost as if he himself had made some kind of decision about their future relationship. Perhaps he simply didn't know what his plans were for the immediate future. And what was the secrecy surrounding his return to Great Cedars? She would have thought it a foregone arrangement that he came back after his leave of absence for research.

Well, she shrugged philosophically, he obviously doesn't intend to say anything more. She made up her mind to enjoy the last twenty-four hours of her own holiday, which wasn't difficult as she walked with her father over the hills and looked at the grazing sheep. Even when a misty rain set in she wasn't deterred, looking down on the little farmhouse in the valley with real affection; a symbol of the security she had grown up with. Somehow, it gave her own life a kind of new dimension, a kind of comparison, and she knew that she was ready now to go back to the hospital and her work on the wards.

She thought Jonathan just might have phoned when he reached home. But he didn't.

Even her father remarked about it. 'That's Jonathan, I suppose . . .'

'He's probably tied up,' Rachel said quickly. 'After all, he has been away a whole year—and there is still time.'

The phone in the hall distracted them. Rachel's heart leapt. It had to be him.

But it was only another farmer on the other side of the hill wanting to discuss transport for getting the sheep in to market on Monday.

'I can drive you to the hospital tomorrow,' her father said, 'if we leave early afternoon.'

'No, Dad. You have to come all the way back. If you could get me on the train I'll be fine. I just change at Bristol and pick up the connection and I'll be back in the nursing block by seven at the latest.'

'If you're sure . . .'

'Of course I am. But thanks. I shall have to do something about getting another car though,' she ended on a note of resignation.

At eight o'clock on Monday morning Rachel stepped out of the lift and walked quickly along the corridors of the orthopaedic floor. Past Sister's office, which she noticed was empty, past the various six-bed wards, to the three-sided enclosed space where all the reports were written up and the records filing cabinets lined the wall. Behind was the main drugs and dressings room.

Sister Bolton, a junior sister, was going through the night reports and looked up at Rachel's approach.

'Oh, Staff, I'm glad to see you back. Have a good holiday?'

'Fine, thanks. Are we a bit short-staffed this morning? Where is everybody?'

'We're not too bad. Sister Benson will be in at nine. I'm here until twelve. Nurses Gray and Cardy are starting on the beds in Fifteen, Nurse Brook and Nurse Dixon are in Five. It's been one hell of a weekend for emergency admissions. We're almost full. These are for theatre this morning on Mr Harrap's list. If you will take over the pre-meds . . .' Sister Bolton consulted another list. 'These patients are down for X-rays, if you'll organise the porters. Mrs Green in Number Twelve and Samuel Collins in Ten are both for Prosthesis.' She stood up. 'I'll do the drugs round now.' She smiled ruefully. 'Nothing's changed, Staff—it's the medicine as before for us,' she added as the bell buzzed persistently behind them.

'Ward Seven—that'll be Bill.'

'I'll go.'

Rachel breezed into the all-male ward, looking along the row of beds to see who was in distress.

'It's Bill, Nurse. He's been groaning something dreadful.'

'What's the trouble, Bill?' she asked, going over to his bed, recognising him as one of the patients admitted before she left for her holiday. Now he was lying on his operation site, unable to move by himself and in obvious pain.

'I'll get another nurse to help lift you, Bill. Hold on,' she said cheerfully, drawing the curtains around his bed. In a moment she was back with Nurse Gray. 'We may as well get his bed done while we're about it,' Rachel decided, her mind already running ahead to the other tasks which were lined up and must be taken in the right order, regardless of interruptions and emergencies. 'Just give me a hand here, will you?'

Suddenly, she knew that she was truly back on ward

duty and heading the other nurses when decisions had to be taken. When they had finished with Bill, Nurse Gray was dispatched to the first pre-op patient.

'Get Linda Masters, Ward Three, into her theatre gown next, Nurse. Check her wristband. Make sure everything essential is there and correctly. Remove any teeth or jewellery. She had had her bath, I presume?'

'Yes, Staff. Early on.'

'Okay. I'll give her her pre-med at nine-fifteen.'

As she went to collect fresh dressings, Sister Benson, about to go into her office, stopped and beckoned Rachel to join her.

'Glad you're back, Staff. How was your holiday?'

'Fine—thank you, Sister.'

'Good. I might want a chat later,' Sister said.

'Right, Sister.'

'What are you up to now?' Rachel put her in the picture.

'Okay. I'll just go through these,' she said, referring to the papers and letters in her hand, 'then I'll be with you. Sister Bolton is around somewhere, I expect.'

'Yes. I believe she is in Ten and Twelve with a student nurse.'

'Thank you, Staff.'

Rachel was dismissed and hurried back to the patient needing fresh dressings in the ward reserved for the more elderly and incapable ladies on that section.

One certainly needs to be a good psychologist, she thought, not for the first time, as she tried to assess and deal with every different person under her care that day. They ranged from the young men thrown from motor cycles and car accident cases, both men and women, to the older, quieter people and the despairing helplessness of the elderly. She could never make up her mind which was the more heart-rending. Despair in the young, with their lives ahead of them, or in the old, at the end of their days. Most of the time she was able to deal with it in perspective, knowing there were limits and what they were. But on that first day back, nothing was that simple. Neither was it long before her arms and legs were aching from the tasks which couldn't wait and must be dealt with immediately.

'Nurse, I want the bedpan!'

'Nurse, I'm not comfortable.'

'Nurse, my pillows want moving.'

'Nurse, I'm going to be sick.' Readjusting tractions, checking bleeding, investigating anything questionable in a section of between forty and fifty patients with too few nurses, especially senior ones, meant one had no count on the miles traversed in the course of one duty roster. And by midweek, Rachel felt she had never been away—except, of course, for the little cameos which crept into her mind at odd moments when she least expected to be reminded of Jonathan. She felt a little uneasy that he hadn't got in touch with her; not since his rather formal goodbye at the gate of her parents' farmhouse. Even that had been disconcerting.

There were moments between then that made her shudder deliciously in retrospect. Surely it was just a question of time before he gave her something more solid to go on where they were both concerned, some hope that their future could be shared? There was so much just waiting for them—but not on his terms. Not this time. No just picking up where they had left off.

'It's not good enough,' she told him silently as she waited for the phone to ring. Just the sound of his voice would help. Somehow she didn't feel she could phone him at his parents' home. She knew very little about them and as he hadn't suggested it . . .

Suddenly the latent feeling of uncertainly was back. Perhaps he was busy with appointments. And what those were she could only guess. He hadn't told her.

And what about Great Cedars? Not once had she heard his name mentioned on the grape-vine and no one here apparently knew he was back from Canada.

The weekend slid by, and Monday and Tuesday. The surgeons' rounds brought Jonathan's image forcibly nearer. Oh—if only he would walk through the door along with the rest of the retinue of medics and doctors.

Rachel slipped across to the nurses' block for her lunch break, planning to make herself a sandwich and bowl of soup instead of going to the dining-room, needing a short time of quiet and hoping there just might be a letter on the mat. She felt a little desperate to recapture something of their time in Scotland. There could never be anyone else to make her feel this way, surely? She didn't want to go out with any of the other men at the hospital either. Most of them knew that and gave up asking. Books and study were one of her relaxations and had been for the past year. But Jonathan was back now—and the aching need to be with him was back too, tugging at her relentlessly.

She sighed, glancing at the watch on her uniform dress, appalled to find that she had only three minutes left to freshen up and get over to the main building and on duty.

Fortunately, one of the housemen was entering the lift and stopped it for her.

'In a hurry, Staff Nurse?' he asked amusedly, pressing her floor button.

'Mm—Sister Benson doesn't excuse unpunctuality, Dr Redding.'

'Especially in a Staff Nurse,' he finished for her. 'Expected to set an example,' he teased, holding the doors back for her to get out. 'Okay—I'm going along with some lab reports,' he said, falling into step beside her.

From the opposite lifts, Mrs Rowntree was being pushed back from X-ray, still scared by the huge apparatus, managing a wan smile at the sight of a familiar face and the reassuring touch of Rachel's hand on her clenched fingers.

'Cheer up, Emily. It's all over now,' she told her brightly and Sister Benson, sitting writing at the desk, looked up and closed the folder, perfectly aware that Rachel was almost five minutes late back.

'Perhaps you'll take charge now, Staff Nurse, until Sister Bolton returns from her lecture,' she said cryptically, giving Dr Redding a straight look as he went to the X-rays and filing cabinet.

'I'll just see Emily into bed, Sister,' Rachel said quietly.

'Oh, yes. Two new patients have been admitted and will be up from Casualty in about an hour. Dr Kratz is coming with them. Both male. Ward Five, I think. It might mean a bit of shifting around so see what you can do, Staff. I'm off now.'

Sister Benson would be back punctually at four o'clock. Until then, it was a question of coping. Rachel glanced at the clock on the wall. It promised to be a rather busy afternoon ahead with the depleted nursing staff. Still, there had been worse times, she thought, as she went in with Emily.

Fortunately the two new patients arrived at the same time as Sister Bolton, which greatly simplified the procedure of getting them into bed and their tractions set up. Aged eighteen and nineteen respectively, Peter and Roy were lucky to be alive.

Contusions of face and limbs were only a part of their injuries. There were two broken legs for Peter, and Roy would need skin grafting once his back could take it. He also had knee injuries and a fractured arm.

'What happened to you?' Sister Bolton asked as they

made them as comfortable as possible. Peter gave her a mournful glance. 'Took the bend too fast, didn't he?' he said disgustedly.

It was a familiar tale on Orthopaedics.

Sister Bolton sighed as they came out. 'They'll never learn, will they?' Glancing up at the clock she gasped, 'Heavens! It's three-thirty already. What about a cup of tea, Staff? Unless you want your break?'

'No. I'll put the kettle on. Sister's back. I'll just see if she would like one . . .'

The student nurse reported back too, so that meant there were three others to attend to the more menial tasks for a few minutes, and then they must get stuck into the dressings again and, after that, the drugs trolley —and all this to be completed before supper at six. A few visitors were sitting with relatives in the various wards and this helped things along a little. There were less calls.

But by eight, when Rachel finally went off duty, she barely knew how to put one foot before the other.

The leaves were already coming off the trees. She felt them scuffle underfoot as she crossed the lawns to the red brick building which seemed a haven just then. There were lights in some of the windows. The evenings were already drawing in fast and there was an autumn nip in the air too, and she pulled her navy cardigan closer around her.

If only there was a letter or a phone call, somehow it would not be such a bleak outlook; but suddenly there seemed nothing to look forward to. Except the rest of the evening. A bath and television—Rachel had her own portable. She was much too exhausted to think of studying tonight. It had been quite a day.

Next morning she felt completely different. She couldn't think why. Simply the aftermath of a good night's rest, probably. But there was a definite lightness in her step as she went across to the main hospital building with a staff nurse from Medical.

'The new children's wing is coming along fast,' the other nurse observed, looking up at the windows where already there were new curtains and animal motifs to be seen.

'Not before time,' Rachel agreed. 'It is badly overdue. I wonder who's staffing it.'

'Mr Gerard, of course, and Dr Barenat are the consultants. But I'm not sure who will be taking the residential posts. I expect it's all settled—just not confirmed yet. You're still on Ortho, aren't you?'

Rachel nodded. 'Yes. I can't see me making any move until I get my Advanced—I'm working at it.'

It was a bright, sunny morning and this, Rachel felt, had to account for her uplift in spirits today. She was even humming as she went up in the lift. Sister Benson, too, seemed in a good mood this morning as she got everything organised quickly and went from bed to bed seeing for herself how the inmates were feeling.

After her morning round-up, as she called it, when she read the night report to her staff and made sure they knew about each individual patient before continuing further, she called Rachel back.

'I am to see Miss Bland in ten minutes. Something's come up. Carry on for me. I shall be back soon. Oh, here's Dr Kratz—I expect she wants to see the new boys. Just ask if she needs you, Staff.'

Which Rachel would have done anyway, she thought, as she went along to Ward Five. She was relieved when Dr Kratz shook her head. 'No, I'm okay—for the moment, anyway,' she murmured as she took the charts from the end of the first bed and studied them.

In Ward Fourteen there were six patients and in the corner bed a tiny little lady of ninety years, who was now calling for a nurse.

'Yes, I'm here, Lucy. What is it?' Rachel responded.

Lucy was already sitting out in her chair, delicately featured and still very fussy about her appearance. She had come in after a fall, with a fracture of her left arm, and quite badly bruised. But once the shock was over, she was progressing remarkably well. She treated the nurses like children, especially when they had to be firm with her.

'Don't you tell me what I will or will not do,' she had told Rachel the previous day. 'I'm old enough to be your grandmother; remember that, my girl!'

Now she asked in a whisper for the commode and Rachel quickly drew the curtains around her bed.

'Go away, please,' Lucy told her firmly. Rachel waited a short time before peeping through the drawn curtains.

'Are you ready, Lucy?'

In no uncertain terms she was told, '*go away*! And do not come back until I ring my bell. Have the nurses no regard for privacy?'

The phone rang on the desk in the corridor and, designating Nurse Gray to stay around in the ward just in case Lucy attempted to get up, Rachel went to answer it, and from there to assist in getting a patient into bed from Recovery. She was adjusting the drip when the crash came. Lucy had fallen out of the commode chair and was face down on the floor.

No one was to blame. Elderly patients needed to have their dignity preserved as far as possible and Nurse Gray was within calling distance. There had been no warning and Lucy might just have nodded off.

'I'd only just that moment looked in at her,' Nurse Gray reported, and the other patients bore this out also.

Lucy had cuts to her nose and chin and it hadn't improved her arm. Dr Redding came at once and the patient was treated for shock and installed in bed once more.

'It should never have happened,' Sister Benson said severely next morning, when she had them all together. 'When a nurse is told to keep an eye on a patient, it means just that, with or without their being aware of it. We all need a dozen pairs of hands and we can't be in two places at once, but this is what is expected of us, so go to it.'

She was tying her own plastic apron as she spoke, and glanced at Rachel. 'I want a word, Staff. Wait, will you?'

Was it because she was late yesterday? Or a further wigging over Lucy? But Sister's first words soon dispelled that.

'I'm afraid I'm going to lose you,' she said wryly. 'Miss Bland wants to see you at twelve.'

'Do you know what it is about?' Rachel asked, mystified.

'Yes. But it has to come from her.'

What on earth could it be? Obviously a move—but where? Rachel pondered.

Punctually at twelve she arrived outside the door of the Chief Nursing Officer's room, her heart beating a little faster than usual as she was told to go in, after knocking. A fresh white cap had been hurriedly pinned in place on her neat, shining hair. The blue and white striped dress was cinched by her purple belt and silver buckle and Miss Bland's eyes ran assessingly over the neat figure and black ward shoes.

'Sit down. I expect you're wondering why I've sent for you.'

That was a catch question, but Rachel couldn't give away any information she didn't know about, so she waited.

'I'll come straight out with it then. I want you to

transfer to the new children's wing in two weeks' time. I am also upgrading you to Junior Sister, under Charge Sister Mitchel. I know you like working in Paediatrics and you will have ample scope for further study in this field. Have you started any advanced work yet?'

Rachel told her that she had, her mind boggling.

'Good. It will be quite a challenge, but the conditions are excellent. You should go over there and have a good look round. Out-patients' clinics are all under one roof now, of course. I think you'll get along with Sister Mitchel and the rest of the staff.'

'I have worked with Sister Mitchel before, ma-am.'

'Good. Well, here are the details of salary etc, which we will go into . . .'

When all these had been discussed and Rachel dismissed, she shook her head disbelievingly as she went back along the corridors and down to the Ortho level.

It was wonderful news. She felt stimulated, her body responding to the exciting lifting of her jaded spirits. Oh, if she could only share her good news with Jonathan! But he was obviously no longer interested and didn't want to know.

When she rang home that night her mother asked if she had heard anything from him.

'No. I expect he's very occupied,' Rachel said generously. 'I just thought you'd like to know you have to call me Sister Woods now.'

The following day, Friday, she was with Dr Redding in Ward Five, hooking up Peter's traction pulley, when she heard footsteps which sent shivers along her spine and even to her fingertips. They came down the corridor and into Sister's office. Then the door closed. It couldn't be, of course—yet her pulses had leapt to answer the intuitive certainly that they were Jonathan's.

Quite probably, though, a visitor or a doctor, she sighed.

'Comfortable?' she asked the young, good-looking Adonis in the bed.

Peter grimaced. 'What do you think?' Dr Redding had disappeared.

'I know. Stupid question, wasn't it? But this is a necessary form of torture, unfortunately. We do want that leg to be right this time.'

'Sure, I know. Only it's me left one . . .' He grinned at his own joke, then resolutely put on his earphones. Rachel left him to a world of pop music which seemed an essential part of his day. Roy was asleep with his headphones still on. She switched them off and went to write her notes.

Dr Redding had gone, yet Rachel was sure she had heard him a moment before, talking at the end of the corridor. She had intended asking him about a test result they were waiting for.

'Rachel . . .'

She glanced up and saw Jonathan. He was standing on the other side of the table, grinning down at her startled expression.

'So it *was* you,' she said softly.

'Was? You mean, it *is*—don't you?'

She didn't say that she had recognised his footsteps a moment ago.

'Sorry I haven't been in touch,' he said seriously. 'But I waited to have something definite to tell you. When are you free?'

'At seven.'

'Oh, a long way off. But I've got a few ends to tie up here first.'

Her heart plummeted. So he wasn't coming back.

'Look, I'll pick you up at seven-thirty and we'll go somewhere for a bite. I have to be back in Bath tonight though.'

'Give me time to change,' she begged.

'Sure. I'll wait. See you, honey.'

He was gone. His echoing footsteps brought a tender smile to her lips as she wondered why they were recognisable only to her. But now she needed a mental shake and Jonathan was excluded from her mind as she went to help the porter return a newly-plastered patient to his bed.

From then on it was all go. If only, she mused, as she answered a constantly buzzing bell, one could just get on with the things that have to be done. She was longing to have a go at the linen cupboards. Instead, she and the other nurses on duty were scurrying hither and thither like scalded cats. It was the frustrating hold-ups which were so taxing and certainly there was no time to indulge her curiosity as to why Jonathan had been at the hospital today.

But the secret joy because she was seeing him tonight lent wings to her feet, and when Sister returned from her tea break it had turned into a beautiful day; even if it was autumnly misty outside and the leaves were falling from the trees in rust and gold showers to lie trembling on the grass.

Jenny Dee, a staff nurse from the children's floor right at the top of the building, carried her cup of tea and slice of yellow cake over to Rachel's table before sitting down heavily and stretching her legs luxuriously under it.

'Dr Paget is back from Canada. Did you know? I think he's coming back here again.'

'Why do you think that?' Rachel asked.

'I heard Mr Gerard telling Sister Carruthers—and I'm sure he said as Senior Registrar. It's just been made official.'

'Good for him,' Rachel said drily, getting to her feet. 'I expect we shall all know in good time. I must get back.'

She didn't intend to volunteer the information that she too was going to transfer to Paediatrics and as Junior Sister. But her thoughts were very clear as she went up in the lift to Ortho. So, that was his news. What a pity that she had to hear on the grape-vine. Perhaps he hadn't thought her sufficiently important to be the first to know. And that hurt.

But he had come to find her today and now she knew why he was hugging his news. After all, it hadn't been confirmed on the board yet. She was acting churlishly.

I suppose I know but can't accept that Jonathan's relationships are very secondary in his life and always will be, she decided, as she reported back for duty. There were still three hours to go before she was off.

A letter lay on the mat of her bed-sitting room when she dashed in at ten past seven. It was from Heather. She and Jeff now had a son. *He is to be called Ewan. He arrived on the 18th, by Caesarean Section. Trust me to be difficult! Isn't it super about Jonathan's pending appointment as Senior Registrar in the new children's wing? I know is isn't actually official yet, but he will obviously accept. You must be over the moon. Are we to hear wedding bells? Mrs McAllister is progressing, Jeff tells me. She's still here on Ortho—and her baby son is getting stronger each day. Thanks for all your back up at this end. Bye now. Love from us all, Heather. P.S. Ewan has red hair—like me.*

Oh, what a day! Rachel mused as she went into the bathroom and began to scrub, before she could think of make-up.

When she emerged from the nurses' home, Jonathan was already waiting. It had taken her just ten minutes to slip into her cream dress and wool coat and run quickly down to the forecourt. The car door was already open and she slid in beside him, aware immediately of his particular male scent and soap. He had brushed his unruly hair across his forehead and he looked tanned and very craggily male as he searched her face, his eyes, oh-so devilishly unreadable.

'Hi, there. Were you late off duty?' he enquired.

'No. I stayed to read Heather's letter.'

'Oh, so you know they have a son?'

'Yes, I do now.' Rachel fastened her seat-belt. 'I seem to be the last to know anything of importance around here. Where are we going?' she asked quickly.

'Rachel . . .' His voice was low and deliberate and thrilled her with its deep intonation. At the same time he reached lazily for her hand. 'Calm down, will you? Relax for once. You're coming out with me for the evening, remember?'

'Oh dear, that's not a very good start, is it?' she asked shakily.

He had to let her hand go then, because of a gear change, but his answer was definite. 'No—it isn't.'

'And I have so much to tell you.'

He smiled, giving her hand a quick squeeze. 'Okay, we'll go to the Green Dragon. Then we can talk. I have much to tell you too.'

She was silent as he took the road leading into the quietness of the country and she watched the trees shadowing the way ahead, until he pulled into the car park of the old pub and the wheels crunched to a halt on the gravel. It was still comparatively early and they were able to find a quiet corner of the lounge, choosing to sit on an old oak settle which had been chosen many times before by two people wanting to be undisturbed.

'This is nice,' she murmured, sitting down on the chunky cushions.

'I think you need a gin and tonic,' he observed and, without waiting, went straight up to the bar.

She was touched by his caring manner after the rather confusing day. Her legs and back ached from the constant manoeuvring around of the patients, most of them immobile and having to be manipulated or simply lifted bodily. But she could shut off now because Jonathan was there, waiting for their drinks—so infinitely dear.

She feasted her eyes on the back of his head, the erect shoulders. Did he have any idea how much she loved him? How much she needed his love in return? Why couldn't she just accept what he had to offer on his terms? Why couldn't she just live for today, taking their normal passions for granted? Was she afraid of losing him again?

He caught the look in her eyes as he came back to her with their drinks, and although it was quickly gone and replaced by a disarming smile, he asked lightly, 'Something on your mind, Rachel? What was your news?'

'Just that I'm to be transferred to the children's block.' She waited for his reaction, which came at once.

'That's wonderful news, because I am taking up a new appointment on the first as Senior Registrar there.'

He waited for her response—and she didn't let him down. 'That's wonderful, Jonathan,' she said sincerely.

'It opens up a whole new concept for me,' he said enthusiastically. 'At last I can become involved. And care of children, as you know, is specialised at any level. Medics either drift through their stint on Paediatrics or take up the challenge—and that's the way I saw it right from the start. I do feel that the nursing staff should be there by choice, though. It's so different from adult nursing and needs a different approach.'

'You're preaching to the converted,' she told him, a new note of understanding in her voice. 'Now, can I finish the rest of my news? Because there's just a chance you may not approve. From the first of the month I'm being upgraded—and I will be Sister Woods then. So we have some cause to celebrate tonight, I would have thought. Aren't you pleased?'

She was watching his face and saw the small lines each side of his mouth deepen.

'Of course I'm pleased,' he said huskily. 'I just don't know how I'm going to see you every day, and not . . .'

'Not what?' Rachel asked softly, her lovely eyes responding to his as he moved closer on the seat.

'Stop flirting with me, Sister Woods,' he murmured against her ear. 'Finish your drink. I think our table is ready.'

'Oh, are we eating here?'

'We are. And we're celebrating—though I mustn't lose sight of the fact that I'm driving back to Bath tonight. Unfortunately . . .'

Tonight she was happy. Tomorrow didn't matter any more. Sister Woods had acquired a new image as she went into the dining-room with Dr Paget at her side.

CHAPTER SIX

JONATHAN'S gaze was reflective as he said, 'We're moving into winter rather earlier this year, it seems. There's quite a nip in the air tonight.'

'Yes, I thought so too. This is a rather nice room, isn't it? I haven't been here since it was refurbished.'

'They do a good menu here too.' He handed her one, running his eyes down the assortment of hot and cold foods. 'What do you fancy?'

'The sole, I think. And no starter.'

'Right. I'll skip that too. They do a good curried beef here. I'll settle for that.'

Having given their order he leaned towards her confidentially. 'I hope we're going to be able to meet like this often, Rachel. Sometimes our off-duty periods must coincide, surely. It's always a bit more difficult when one is in residence, of course, but maybe we'll have to work at it.' Then, after a moment, he added roguishly, 'You'll just have to come calling, won't you? My flat actually boasts a tiny kitchen and shower, and my bed-sit is pleasantly impressive.'

'Is that wise?' Her dark eyes were raised to his now.

'For you to visit? Why not? I do have some privileges you know, and I shall entertain from time to time. I'm not expected to live monastically, for heaven's sake. It's certainly more private on my floor than the nurses' block, that's for sure. But then you'll be moving over to the other building now, of course.'

'The sisters' house, yes. I shall also hope to be studying this winter. The new paper being introduced for a post-registration in Paediatrics is a must, I feel; and, like you, a new promotion does lend fresh impetus to everything one does. So I suppose I'm all set to get started.'

'Rachel,' he said sternly, 'we have to unwind sometimes. You and me, both . . . You know what the pressures are. Sick children can play hell with one emotionally as well as physically, and there's no way to prevent that happening other than switching off. A residency precludes that, because when I'm on duty I'll be on call night and day quite often and I'll have to be involved. Certainly from a nursing standpoint it can be even more difficult, I imagine.'

'Let's not talk shop,' Rachel said dreamily as their food arrived; the wine had already relaxed her and she was desperately trying to unwind after the unusual day behind her.

Jonathan drove them both swiftly back to the hospital afterwards because it was late when they finished their coffee and came out into the misty, crisp air. It was a dark night, but the sprinkling of stars way up above lent an illusion of brightness.

'You won't mind if I don't see you to the door, will you?' he said softly, drawing her close after the engine was switched off.

'Of course not. You still have quite a drive ahead of you.'

Her words were smothered in the force of his mouth on hers; the passions behind his kisses bruising her lips.

'Jonathan . . .' she gasped breathlessly, feeling her own urgent responses rising too, having made no effect to repress them.

'Hell!' he ground out savagely, reluctantly releasing her. 'See what you do to me? I must be crazy to let you out of my sight.'

'I agree,' she laughed lightly, teasingly laying her

flushed cheek against his before their mouths clung again.

'What am I going to do about you, Rachel?' he muttered, holding her face in his hands while his eyes gleamed in the half-light, reminding her again of a tiger in the dark.

'What do you want to do about me?' she asked in a whisper.

'Oh God, why must you make life so complicated? You know what you're doing to me, yet you . . .'

Now she giggled helplessly. He knew the reason why. He stopped her forcibly, covering her mouth with kisses and holding her so close that she could feel the heat of him through his shirt. And as she lost herself in the exquisite yearning she longed for him to say, just once, that he loved her—not simply wanted her. *That* she knew already. Until he actually said those words, she couldn't either. Not after that last time in the hotel room at Gretna.

It gave her the needed strength to draw away and put her hand on the door handle, which broke the spell.

Her ran his fingers through his hair and took a deep breath.

'Good night,' she said softly. 'I must let you go. It was a lovely evening, but everything good seems to come to an end too soon,' she ended ruefully.

'Glad you enjoyed it.' He spoke in a near normal voice, perhaps wondering how she had switched off so abruptly and why, and following her example.

'Good night then,' she said again.

'Good night, Rachel—I . . .' He hesitated, as if about to say something more, then his expression sharpened as he had second thoughts. 'I'll see you around. I shall be in and out of the new wing during the week.'

She smiled, closing the car door, and he started up at

once. Before she even reached the gates he was out of earshot.

'You had better be warned,' she told herself firmly as she climbed the stairs to her room without meeting anyone. 'You're going to have to be careful in future. Jonathan has to come across first.'

She wanted reassurance from him because he knew very well how she felt towards him and unless they were extra-vigilant when they saw each other every day, then everyone else would too. And the last thing she wanted the grape-vine to pick up was that Sister Woods and Dr Paget had something going. Although they had been involved before he went to Canada, things could change in a year and anyway, only Heather knew the depth of the liaison.

Rachel missed Heather very much because she hadn't any special girl associates with whom she could talk privately. She was now between confidantes. Not that she ever had been one to discuss her very private affairs at any time. It was just that she and Heather had started out on that lowest rung of the ladder together and had seen each other through some tearful moments those first months.

Rachel decided to write to her soon, but not right now. Because tonight had belonged to she and Jonathan, and had been rather wonderful, she mused, as she thankfully stretched her limbs down into the cool sheets. Just being together, watching his face, his mannerisms, meant so much. And his kisses drew her very soul to the surface.

Dear God—how she loved him. Why, oh why, couldn't she just simply give in to their need of each other? Accept what he had to give on his terms and see what happened? Did she have to be so prissy? Sometime there might be a new woman in his life and Jonathan may even want to marry her. Wouldn't she regret the opportunities she had thrown away? Like the perfect setting at Gretna?

No . . . No . . . Her whole mind recoiled from that thought. Rachel pushed it aside, sure that for her this way was the right one. There would be more regrets if they had just an affair on his terms.

Only she wanted him so much. There could never be any man to take Jonathan's place in her heart. Rachel fell asleep with the exciting prospect of working with him all winter and a future that was still hers to shape in any way she wanted.

Next day there was a letter from Mrs McAllister. Her baby son was improving all the time now. *He is just adorable*, she wrote. *My husband brings the girls to see him and they can't wait to take him home. I am getting around on crutches and longing to walk properly again. I owe you so much, Nurse. If it wasn't for you and your lovely doctor, we might not have him. God bless you—I still think he sent you to me.*

'Oh, dear . . .' Rachel felt the tears in her eyes before she was aware how much the words had affected her. She remembered, in detail, that cottage with all its privations and felt very humble as she buckled her belt around her waist and prepared to start another day on the wards. That was what nursing was really all about after all. Not glamorous at any time or in any situation. Simply basic; helping any sick person in need, whether it be a child, man or woman. And against that thought even Jonathan was relegated to second place today, as she went out into the grey morning and across the dewy grass to the main hospital building.

Meeting up with Jan Shaw, a second-year nurse on Ortho, she had to hear about last night's tiff with her boyfriend which was the cause of today's depths of despair.

'Don't worry,' Rachel advised cheerfully, 'just give

him time to cool off. They all want their own way, but if he's worth his salt he'll be back, Jan. You'll see.'

'Oh, I'm glad I ran into you, Staff—I feel better already.'

'Good. Because we've got quite a day ahead of us. Consultants' round and later the ops, and somehow it all puts other things into perspective, doesn't it? Have you done your hair again?' She eyed the other girl's topknot of twisted hair pinned in a coil. 'That chestnut colour really does something for you.'

'Oh, don't! That's what started it all. Bob liked the gold better—and I was late turning up and he said I looked like a film star gone wrong . . .'

'Oh, no . . .' Rachel couldn't repress a smile as they divested themselves of their cloaks in the changing room. But once on the wards, as she tied a plastic apron over her dress before getting stuck into the bed rounds, she wondered how she could so glibly give advice to another nurse when she couldn't even sort out her own love-life.

The red light was on and the buzzer with it. The next moment she was off down the corridor to answer it. Her day had started.

Jonathan came into the hospital twice before actually taking up residence. He was involved with the new apparatus being installed and getting the feel of it all, but not actually starting in the clinic until Monday morning. He would work under the paediatric consultants and over the housemen.

She heard someone say that Dr Paget had taken a hand in planning the facilities over on the new wing, and had incorporated some of the developments he had picked up in Canada, his ideas having apparently been taken seriously by his colleagues and Administration. All this was news to Rachel.

But Jonathan actually called on the house phone

on her last day on Orthopaedics and asked for her by name.

'Sister Woods,' the new junior eyed her respectfully, 'Dr Paget for you.'

'Hi there, Rachel . . .' Even his voice did things to her, though her tone was carefully controlled. 'Can you spare an hour? I want to show you the new set-up over here.'

'But . . .'

'No buts—when are you free?'

'Now, actually. I was just going for a late lunch.'

'Do you need it?'

'Not really.'

'I'd like you to get a preview,' he urged.

'I'll come now,' she said, unaware that her voice told him a great deal.

As her promotion was now confirmed, she walked through the corridors leading from the main building to the children's department wearing the dark blue dress and frilled cap depicting her new status just a little self-consciously. Rachel was beginning to realise that there was a very big difference in status and that while something had been gained, quite a lot had been lost for ever. She was going to have to adjust to the new image, which was why it was a good thing to be changing departments. One couldn't suddenly change towards one's nurses, not when there had been close confidences exchanged and little friendships and other intimate commiserations, and general helping each other out. Now she was just a little bit on the other side of the fence. As yet it didn't show, but she must adjust to her new image.

She found Jonathan behind a desk in his room. On the door, in black letters was a sign: Senior Registrar. Dr Jonathan Paget.

He got up at once. 'Hi, there—you look very impressive,' he said in greeting, adding, in a sexy whisper, 'very delectable too, Sister Woods . . .'

Rachel blushed helplessly. 'Don't do this to me,' she hissed between clenched teeth.

'Why not? I like seeing that rosy hue,' he said irrepressibly. 'I shall seize every opportunity.'

'Not if we are to work together,' she told him firmly.

'Rachel, you know I'm teasing!' Jonathan protested.

'Then don't—while we're on duty.'

'You're not. Aren't you supposed to be lunching? Do you want something? Coffee?' he offered.

'No. I came because you wanted to show me the lay-out. Is this supposed to be my initiation?'

'Well, I would have thought Sister Mitchel might have done that. She's been over this morning. But come and check things out. I've got half an hour.'

'Well,' she began doubtfully, 'I'm not officially supposed to be here until Monday morning.'

'Come with me . . .'

Walking beside him, hearing his measured footsteps on the newly-laid flooring, purposeful, confident, only succeeded in giving her butterflies. Jonathan in his new professional guise was making her nervous, which was unthinkable. Perhaps it was due to the fact that she was, as yet, unfamiliar with the new format and lay-out, and until the wheels were oiled and the new wing running smoothly, it would be a little difficult for them all.

But with sick children in their care, every nurse would be working all out to make the move as untraumatic as possible. In fact, some of the less ill children might actually enjoy it.

'This is the general waiting room,' Jonathan said, leading her inside.

'Oh—it looks exciting.' There were long, attractive curtains at the wide windows and sun blinds. The walls were pale on three sides, but the other was a cool green-blue. There were several prints.

'Disneyland in miniature,' Rachel observed, 'and that end is rather like stepping into the Space Age. The little patients won't be able to wait to get here. That was clever of someone.'

'My idea, actually. It does work. Especially when these kids have to wait—perhaps when Mr Gerard is seeing them for the first time. The diagnosing runs on a bit unavoidably, then they get impatient, even raucous, and it can turn into a circus, as you know. But get them interested and they forget the time. The atmosphere helps. There are still the more usual books and games and toys, of course, for the less adventurous. The change-over starts on Monday.'

'So do I.'

'As if I'd forgotten that! I think you should have been more involved before then. You're going to be thrown in at the deep end.'

He drew a deep breath, looking round the large room, speculating, Rachel noticed, with some pride before his face became serious again. 'We're in for a hectic time, I guess, even without emergencies.'

'The mothers will probably help. The serious ones stay in, don't they?'

'Some do—others can't. I suppose from one aspect it's good to know they are on call. Others are best not here at all. Experience has taught me a lot in the past and I have reservations.'

'I know. I shall be glad to get over here now. It's a challenge and I can't wait, as I've already said. You are already in residence?'

He nodded. 'Yes. And I've mountains of paperwork to get through. Officially I'm on this evening, which means through the night, too, if I'm needed.'

'I'm glad you've made it,' she said softly. 'Bye.'

Their eyes met, just for a second. His were unreadable. But as she turned to walk swiftly away from their disturbing effect, Rachel realised that she was going to have to do something about that. How different life would be from now on, working closely with the man she loved, watching him with the small patients; sharing his anxieties, his successes. His frustrations too, because there would be plenty of those from day to day.

Even thinking about Jonathan sent the exciting little tremors running riot again through her upright, beautifully slim body which she usually forgot about, unless his nearness reminded her that she was every inch a woman with a natural woman's instincts. Also that she was twenty-four years old, which was perhaps why it was a little awesome to have suddenly become a senior when she least expected it. She had to accept the fact that her promotion, of necessity, carried some reserve along with it.

On Sunday evening, Rachel moved her clothes and books and personal things over to the sisters' section; a two-storied building on the other side of the drive, boasting its own lawn and flower border behind it. Her room was on the upper floor and she could just see the rooftops and surrounding hills around Gloucester from her window. Now she felt very much the way she had as a junior, moving into a first-year hostel, except that her new quarters were a definite improvement and even boasted a shower and wash-basin of her own, besides other facilities hitherto unknown. It was furnished with white melamine fitted cupboards and there were two armchairs. The bed looked as if it might prove very comfortable and there was even a small table for the white portable TV her parents had given her for her twentieth birthday.

Sister Benson had wished her well, admitting that she

was parting with her with great reluctance. 'But,' she added briskly, 'I'm convinced it's the right move for you. Time you moved on. You'll get on fine on Paediatrics; I almost envy you, except that one needs to be a bit younger than me to get on to the present-day juvenile wavelength. It won't be easy, Rachel, but you've earned your promotion and it's now up to you.'

'Thank you for all your help, Sister. I won't let you down,' Rachel said huskily.

'Let's not start getting emotional. Just take one day at a time. You'll find it's an entirely different pair of shoes you're wearing as Sister Woods. Takes a little time to adjust. Good luck. Oh, my room is on the ground floor. Number fourteen—if you need anything.'

'I appreciate that. Thanks.'

In the kitchen a bottle of sherry was soon disposed of and the nurses had also clubbed together and given Rachel a white vase filled with bronze chrysanthemums. Now she sat and admired them, looking round her room with pride. And tomorrow she would be working with Jonathan. She wondered idly whether she should phone him but decided against it. He could easily contact her if he wished to do so. She doubted if he was even free. She hadn't seen him since Friday lunch-time.

Before she went to bed she phoned home, speaking to her parents in turn and being left in no doubt how delighted they were at her promotion.

'And Jonathan?' her mother queried.

'Senior Registrar on Paediatrics. So you see, I shall be working with him quite a lot.'

'Well, well. Do you get leave soon?' her mother wanted to know.

'I shouldn't think so,' Rachel laughed, 'but I've got to do something about getting myself a small car—I really need one.'

'Have you got enough money?'

'I can manage, I think. Just. My salary is increased now somewhat.'

'I see. Well, don't mind asking for a loan,' her father put in, obviously glued to her mother's ear.

She laughed lightly. 'Thanks, Dad. Not necessary, I'm sure, but you are a dear to think of it.'

She slept better than she probably would have done but for that short conversation with them. It balanced things out a bit, besides giving her the assurance that they were there, in the background, ready to help—putting up with her independence, perhaps admiring it, but hoping that she just might need something from them sometime.

Monday morning was a day she never forgot. She was involved in a way she had never been previously and soon realised that ner newly-acquired uniform carried more power than she had imagined.

The change-over had begun. Porters and every available pair of hands were transporting apparatus, trolleys, drip stands, boxes of dressings, dispensary stock, file cabinets, cots, beds, piles of linen—everything, in fact, that was relevant to the move.

Sister Mitchel was in charge. A good organiser, she came from her office with a list in her hands, stopping to wait for Rachel as a huge truck-load of bed linen passed her in the corridor.

'Good morning, Sister Woods. I'm glad you came up early. There's plenty to do. Welcome to what I can only describe as a corner of bedlam this morning. Round up the other nurses, will you? We'll have a quick résumé,' she instructed a passing junior, before turning back to Rachel.

'Dr Paget has been over to go through the Kardex with Dr Roper. I suggest you do the same as soon as you can, before it disappears.'

A flushed bevy of nurses gathered around the centre table in the corridor.

'This is Sister Woods, who is joining us from today,' she told the assembled girls. 'She has come from Ortho. Now, I'll just run through this quickly. Patients—we'll move one ward at a time and that way we shall achieve some semblance of order. Hopefully, too, there will be no emergencies, but you all know what to do if there are. Dr Paget and Dr Roper are on call. In fact, they've been helping here this morning.'

Rachel glanced at the brooches pinned on the nurses' print dresses, stating their names. Their status she knew from the belts they wore. Her own silver buckle and cap, together with the navy-blue dress, were still so new that she felt alienated from them already. Decision-making was part of the duties of a staff nurse, but on a vastly different level when one reached Sister status. And handling children, especially tiny ones, was different in every way from the larger limbs of the adults on Ortho.

Rachel took charge of her first small patient, a two-year-old boy admitted with pneumonia, but with a much more serious condition, now tentatively diagnosed. Sister Mitchel briefed her.

'Dr Paget wants an EMG later today. He suspects amyotonia, I'm afraid, though how this little chap has got this far without it being discovered, I can't imagine.'

Rachel winced. 'I'll take him then.' She noticed at once the flaccid muscles in the little body, also his difficulty in getting muscle response with each breath. And he was only the first problem child in that endless day.

Jonathan became a part of it. As his clinic was on Tuesdays and Fridays, Mr Gerard had come into the hospital for emergency surgery. It was also his day to see his private patients who he was fitting in somehow.

Everyone worked like Trojans and the transfer was completed at break-neck speed, as porters helped push the children, some of whom really enjoyed being propelled along the corridors at top speed, to the new wards.

As Sister Mitchel was in supreme command of the nursing staff, Rachel found herself assigned to the needs of the more seriously ill little ones, together with a second-year nurse.

Twice during the afternoon Jonathan was called and once he answered his bleep to the houseman in Casualty to advise on a ten-year-old boy injured in a cycle accident and comatose.

That same evening they operated to save the boy's life. Rachel didn't see him again until next day. Sister Burnett was doing a night duty and it was she who saw him into bed when he was released from the recovery room. By then Rachel had handed over and dragged her legs up to her room with little in the way of responses left. But there was an enormous feeling of satisfaction to compensate. Satisfaction at a job well done by all the dedicated people in her profession who cared, and at her own stretching powers to meet every task that had been asked of her since early morning.

As she drew her curtains across the window she could see the new wing, its lighting subdued now, blending with the darkness, and then up to the top floor where Jonathan's window was in darkness too. She wondered where he was at that moment. Beneath his window the tree branches swayed as a fresh wind came in from the hills. Oh, how lovely it was, here in this setting. How lucky she had been to train here, reasonably close to home. For some reason, a childhood recollection returned. Her parents had taken her to London for a day and they had gone on a river trip to the Tower. When they disembarked at Westminster Bridge, she had seen the nurses across the river at one of the windows of a tall building.

'That's St Thomas's,' her mother told her in answer to her query.

'Then that is where I shall go to learn to be a nurse,' she had said decisively.

And her father's tolerant, 'You'll need to work a lot harder at school than you're doing now, if you want to have that kind of career, Rachel,' did nothing to dispel the idea, newly born. In fact it acted as a kind of incentive. She set out to come into the top group for the next six years. But St Thomas's became the Cedars, which was much nearer home, and before being accepted Rachel had added three A-levels to her eight O-levels. But as she gazed out into the night, she knew that it had all started there, where the trees lined the river bank. And she permitted herself a little thrill of pride—she had made it, too.

Slipping out of her blue dress and putting it on a hanger, it seemed to symbolise the woman she had become in twelve hours. And although she and Jonathan had only spoken briefly and always professionally that day, they had been in unison as never before.

But she must get some sleep. But how to switch off? Television; a book? She chose the latter and fell asleep over it, with the light still on.

Next morning she was back on duty at eight. For a few days the roster times were going to be a little stretched, mainly because there was so much paperwork to be kept up to date. Sister Mitchel arrived earlier too, but by then Rachel had read through the night reports. There were several really worrying cases. The pneumonia boy was one. She went along to him first.

He lay in his cot, with every symptom of the diagnosed illness. Because of his limp muscles, mucus was slowly filling his lungs and he could not react against it. Today would prove Jonathan right, she thought, when the electroymyogram results were known. Rachel raised the child gently on his pillows, cooling his body as she sponged him. He only wanted to sleep and be left alone, so after a quick word with Jenny Dee, on duty today, she checked the small people in the other beds, most of whom were already washed and made comfortable before breakfast. This, too, was a lengthy business as quite a few children had to be fed. Later, the mothers or even grandmas helped, but it was a little early for them to arrive.

Peter, a child who had been admitted for a transfusion because of leukaemia, gazed up at her listlessly when she stood by his bed. 'Hallo, I'm Sister Woods—remember, I was here yesterday? Do you like your new room?'

He moved his head slightly.

'You don't?'

'I like the curtains and things.'

'So do I.' Her eyes were noticing all the relevant manifestations as they scanned him. 'Have you got a pain, Peter?' she asked gently.

'My head hurts.'

'And your legs?'

He nodded, his mouth trembling as he tried not to cry. 'I want Mummy.'

'Mummy will be in soon,' she told him. 'She promised to come as soon as she has taken your small sister to nursery school. What is your sister called?'

'Jane.'

Jenny Dee, on the other side of the room, came across to them. 'Do you want a hand to sit Peter up a little?' she asked softly.

'Yes. I think we'll get Dr Paget to have a look at him this morning.'

'He's not eating,' Jenny whispered.

'Is your mouth sore, Peter?' Rachel asked, as together

they lifted him into a more comfortable position, turning his pillows as they did so.

He nodded.

'Well, perhaps we can make it a little bit better.'

They left him watching the door for his mother, crossing to the six-year-old girl in the other bed.

'Lucy came in for intravenous therapy,' Jenny explained.

'Yes. I remember this one. She's going home soon, isn't she? The weekend, isn't it?'

'Mmm. Her mother comes when she can. There are twins at home, I believe.'

'Hallo, Lucy. Did you enjoy your ride yesterday?'

She nodded, her eyes dark and huge in the small elfin face. 'My mummy is bringing me a new dress to wear home.'

'Lovely. I wonder what colour it is,' Rachel smiled.

'I don't know. You can see it when she comes.'

'I shall look forward to that,' Rachel said brightly, checking the charts at the end of the bed before going on to the next ward.

When Jonathan came along the corridor later he went straight into Peter's room after noticing that Rachel was re-bandaging a small boy's arm. She joined him as soon as she had finished, for Sister Mitchel was in her office on the phone to someone. He had finished reading the relevant notes and was sitting on the side of Peter's bed, feeling his neck glands gently.

After his examination he looked up at Rachel, his brow furrowed. She knew that Jonathan had noticed Peter's breath, a very tell-tale symptom, as she had earlier. He had drawn the curtains which divided the room, and now he preceded her around them to the other child. Here he made a cursory examination, the facts of her progress in his hands.

'I suggest that Lucy goes home today. One day won't

make much difference. I want Peter to be kept very quiet for the next twenty-four hours. Lucy's mother comes in later, I expect.'

'I can reach her on the phone,' Rachel said quietly.

'Do that, will you?' Jonathan's brow furrowed. She knew why.

'You'll need to keep a very close watch on that small boy, Sister. There's a danger of epistaxis, I think—or worse.'

'I understand, Dr Paget.'

'I believe his mother is already completely in the picture, but if she asks to see me, arrange it, will you?'

Rachel nodded, a lump gathering in her throat. This was something she was going to have to come to terms with. The emotional part of paediatric nursing.

'Apparently, she likes to give him his blanket bath,' she murmured. 'Do you think it should be skipped today? I have sponged him.'

'Yes,' he said briefly. 'Now, I think I'd like a look at Trina while I'm here.' He glanced at his watch. 'I've got two minutes before I'm due in my out-patients' clinic.' He smiled at her as she walked by his side to another ward. 'I expect you feel a bit as I do; not quite grounded yet.'

'We're getting organised very quickly, actually, but I don't have the location of everything under control yet. And these patients are new to me, which means checking and re-checking their case histories. But I'm getting there. Sister Mitchel is a tower of strength.'

'I'm convinced she's glad to have you too.' His white-coated shoulders bent over Trina's cot in the eight-bedded ward, so there was no time to show him she appreciated that. This child had been admitted because of persistent vomiting.

Jonathan straightened up, tickling the little girl under her chin as he did so.

'Give me a little smile then,' he encouraged her. 'You're better today—no smile?' The child closed her eyes, shutting him out, and as he straightened up and went out to the corridor he took Trina's notes with him.

'No more diarrhoea, I see; but I think, as a precaution, she should be isolated. Are there any lab reports back?'

'Some. We're giving the salt, potassium and fluids because of the dehydration, but she isn't retaining them.'

'So we must correct the electrolyte imbalance right away. I'll look in at her this afternoon when, hopefully, we'll have the other results back. We may have to give her a transfusion. There is some rigidity in the neck, did you notice? I'll write up some Neomycin.' He thought for a moment. 'The spinal tap was clear but I have some reservations about this one. Get her isolated, just in case, Sister.'

'I'll get on to it right away,' Rachel said positively. Jonathan unexpectedly smiled into her eyes and all the bells rang.

She heard his steps receding along the corridor; the swing doors close behind him, but she didn't look round.

Checking Peter, she saw with relief that his mother was with him. Then, sitting at the desk, she carefully added Jonathan's observations and new medication to Trina's notes.

Sister Mitchel opened her office door, sailing forth with a sheaf of papers under her arm, coming to a full stop beside her junior sister.

'Thanks for giving me a chance to catch up with this lot,' she said crisply. 'Who did Dr Paget come to see? It's time he was taking clinic.'

'Peter—and he also wanted to check on Trina. Apparently he was called to her during the night.'

'I know. And Peter—does he think he is relapsing?'

'Yes, I think so,' Rachel said quietly. 'So do I.'

'Poor little chap. His mother is here, I see.'

Rachel brought Sister up to date with the new developments on Trina. 'He would like her isolated.'

'Does he suspect meningitis? Polio, for heaven's sake?'

'They're not classical symptoms,' Rachel observed, 'are they?'

'They don't have to be. You'll learn never to rule out anything with these kids. Put her in seven then. And,' she glanced at her watch, 'I shall be off when her mother or father comes in. They're both working parents and I'm off at six tonight, so you'd better have a word with them. Right now, come round with me, Sister Woods, and we'll get our flock into proper perspective. The other nurses can manage without us. Good—I see you've got your pad. Those notes will stand you in good stead. It helps to fit the faces to the names, I find. Just listen to that little lot—you'd never think they were in hospital! More like a zoo . . .'

She stood in the doorway and the pillow fight in progress eased down. Four red-faced boys crept back to their beds.

'Don't,' Sister Mitchel said firmly in her deepest tone, 'let me catch you doing that again.'

Slowly her eyes went from one boy to the next. 'You are put in here together to help cheer each other up a bit—this way you'll soon be segregated. And if you don't know what that word means, look it up when you have a chance. I can hear lunch coming, boys, so simmer down!'

'Yes, Sister,' they chorused in unison.

'You see?' Sister commented. 'Little heathens, aren't they? So don't be too sweet and understanding with them—they'll walk all over you.'

When Rachel reached the sanctuary of her room that

night, she kicked off her shoes and wearily put on some coffee. Then she divested herself of her uniform and had just slipped into a housecoat when Jonathan phoned her room.

'Hi, there. Come up for a drink around nine, will you? I guess we both need it tonight.'

For a moment she couldn't answer. Then, as all her impulses surged towards him, she murmured, 'Jonathan, I'd love to.'

And devilishly he said in his most husky voice, which made her pulses throb—as well he knew—'That's what I hoped you'd say. See you soon, honey.'

As she went up to his room a half-hour later, Rachel hoped that she didn't meet anyone who might possibly misconstrue her intentions in visiting Dr Paget. After all, they were both new to their higher grades; she didn't want the grape-vine to pick anything up yet.

But the moment he opened his door and she saw the subdued lighting in the room behind him, the expression on his face as he closed it again; as soon as she felt his arms enfold her, holding her tightly in a rather desperate hug, nothing seemed to matter any more except the wonderful way he was kissing her.

CHAPTER SEVEN

WHEN they drew apart Rachel had to close her eyes in an effort to recover some semblance of stability. Flushed and a little breathless, she couldn't know that, at this moment, Jonathan might have promised anything to prolong the exquisite delight he was experiencing while holding her so close to him. He reached for her again, control slipping, his voice low and husky with rising passion as he murmured her name.

'Rachel . . . I've wanted to do this all week. Did you know?'

She shook her head, then raised her mouth to his, unable to bear any separation, her whole body dissolving as their limbs moulded together, as if in recognition. She simply gave herself up to that moment of joy and nothing else mattered any more.

But it was short-lived. In the aftermath of warmth and togetherness, he led her towards his tweed-covered settee, impatiently clearing away the books and papers on which he had been working earlier.

A low table was also littered with papers and more textbooks. His table lamp cast its glow into the corners of the room as he went over to a shelf unit to pour drinks for them. He was on his way back, his eyes seeking hers, full of an expression she knew, when the phone bleeped insistently. Grimacing, he answered it at once, his voice already quietly controlled.

'Dr Paget.' After a moment he said, 'I'll be right down.'

'Casualty?' Rachel queried, already on her feet.

''Fraid so. Two children involved in a car crash. They've already alerted theatre staff. Must go, Rachel.'

'Of course. I will too . . .'

He touched her face lightly as they went to the door, switching off at once, and in seconds they were in the lift to the ground floor; and here their ways divided, he disappearing through the swing doors towards Casualty while she went out into the crisp night air and across to the sisters' block.

Part of her thoughts went with him because she didn't need to use much imagination to picture what he would find there. She had to forcibly switch her mind off from that. Tomorrow it would be her job to be responsible for nursing them back to recovery, and that would be the most to hope for. Now, surely, she could allow herself to recapture something of tonight's shared closeness and joy.

Her room looked restful and was her own. She had noticed two of the sisters preparing a meal in the communal kitchen as she came through the entrance, but no one else was around and she didn't mind her own company in the least. Especially tonight.

After she had made coffee and slid thankfully into her armchair, one thought became uppermost in her mind. It was a comforting thought, because she felt tonight that she had seen something more of the man behind Jonathan's mask. Because she knew now that he loved her. She had really seen it tonight in his eyes. It was not simply physical attraction and need. Tonight, those lazy, tigerish eyes, which could spring to awareness, alert to any given situation when the need arose, had given him away. There had to be another reason, other than the one he had used before about not wanting to be committed in any way, why he hesitated to say that he was in love with her too.

And in some ways, neither did she want to commit

herself. Not yet, anyway. But it was good just to know that they belonged together. Emotionally, she pressed her hands to her face, reliving every moment of this evening. The warmth of Jonathan's kisses. The strength of his arms around her, pressing her even closer to his lithe body.

She was behaving like a love-sick teenager. So what? Is there anything wrong with that? she asked herself defensively. Why not, when tonight it coloured her world and brought the sparkle back to her eyes. She felt alive again. Restless, perhaps, but alive and in love.

She decided to write to Heather, feeling too restless for bed yet. There were quite a few bits of news to pass on. Besides, it helped to be able to talk about Jonathan and his work in the new wing. Jeff would be interested too.

And Heather would like to know about the children's ward. She was probably the only person in the world who didn't want explanations and would understand Rachel's need to write out her thoughts sometimes.

The siren of an incoming ambulance distracted her momentarily. It passed her window on the way to Casualty. It never ended; yet another human in need of professional help. So many patients had confirmed that when they were in pain, frightened and sick, it was a relief to get into hospital. And she had chosen to be part of it. Jonathan too. There was comfort and peace in that thought, and in a few minutes Rachel was asleep.

Next morning, Sister Mitchel sought her out after the reports and initial work of the day was under way. Both of the children admitted the night before had needed surgery and both were in an end ward together, opposite the table where they could easily be seen.

'We'll do the ward rounds together this morning, Sister Woods,' her senior said reflectively. 'That way we have an up-to-date progress report of our own.'

Sister Mitchel was very experienced and wise and had seen most of the traumatic situations before, but even she admitted that modern living and science were a little overwhelming. She liked to get right down to the basic reasons behind most problems. There were plenty of those and they were not found in textbooks, either.

There were six beds in the first ward. 'We'll start here,' Sister said, as they stood unobserved in the doorway. In the first one a boy of five lay on high pillows watching the other children, some walking, others sitting up in cots playing with small toys, while two, recovering from surgery, were still sleeping.

'Andrew is still withdrawn,' Sister observed, 'otherwise he seems over the worst.'

He had come in with bronchial asthma which necessitated him being in an oxygen tent for a time. Now, though exhausted, he was showing signs of being more comfortable. They both noticed the way he breathed from his stomach and not his chest, as chronic asthmatics do.

'I do hope he grows out of it,' Sister said quietly. 'Every time he picks up an infection this happens.' She went up to his bed. 'Hallo, Andrew. Feeling a bit better today?'

He didn't respond, turning his head away, his brown eyes looking enormous in the small white face. Rachel saw from his chart that he was responding to the antibiotics, his temperature down.

Sister still looked thoughtful as they moved on to the next bed where a lovely little coloured girl was recovering from one of the collagen diseases, fortunately resolving after bed rest, the rash almost gone now.

'One of her family is here for most of the time,' Sister murmured. 'Happy little thing, isn't she?'

A physiotherapist had come up to Andrew's bed. He looked up, startled, but she quickly reassured him.

'It's all right. I just want you to cough for me, then we're going to do some breathing exercises together. Sit up. That's right. Now—a great big cough if you can.' Meanwhile, she was testing his chest reflexes. 'Good. Now, a deep breath, like this . . .'

'He'll do, I think,' Sister Mitchel said as they left the ward. 'I just wish he wasn't so shut off. There has to be a reason. What on earth is going on behind those watchful eyes, I wonder? He's much too quiet for a boy of his age.'

Rachel had made her own observations and thought she might like to discover the reason for herself. She wasn't yet sure just how deeply she could safely become involved with each small patient. Especially the longer-term ones, or those seriously ill. Even now, at some time, most of the small heads seemed to come to rest on the firm breasts beneath the navy dress when the children were in her arms for support or comfort. Tears were never very far away in a children's ward.

Between the ages of two and five they were most vulnerable. The babies were in a separate ward. Those too were heart-catching. Every child admitted had a problem of some kind, either simple or complicated, and ultimately their care depended on a doctor's decision. But it was the nurse looking after that child who quite often became the mother figure.

Jonathan was in Out-patients this morning with Mr Gerard and Dr Roper, but immediately he was free he came to the ward. Rachel, bringing the records up to date at the table in the corridor, heard his footsteps before he came into view. Sister Mitchel having just gone to lunch, Rachel was in charge.

Putting down her pen, she stood up at once, asking quietly, 'Peter?'

'Yes.' His mouth was set in a firm line, only his eyes betraying his concern. 'Is his mother here?'

'Yes. His father is on his way.'

Jonathan sighed, walking purposefully beside Rachel along to the small ward where Peter's mother looked up from her chair beside the bed. She knew what this relapse meant. There had been unexpected remissions since the leukaemia was first diagnosed two years earlier, but they had always known there was diminishing hope of a cure for Peter as the months passed and he was readmitted to hospital for tests, transfusions and drug therapy from time to time.

Jonathan took the child's wrist in his strong fingers, so sensitive sometimes, as Rachel well knew and, for a moment, there was quiet in the room. Then Peter's father arrived and went straight to his wife. At an almost imperceptible sign from Jonathan, he and Rachel left, leaving them together.

Jenny Dee, who was a staff nurse anyway, was within earshot and if a sister was needed, had only to press a bell. Just now there was nothing more anyone could do for the tired little boy already comatose in the bed.

But for the other patients there were a great many tasks to be got through. Only this morning Jonathan had admitted two children for observation. One was an appendicitis suspect and the other had a bone infection which Mr Gerard suspected could be osteomyelitis at early stage. All the nurses were working full out.

Andrew's grandmother had brought him a chocolate mousse which she had made specially and as he hadn't eaten any lunch Rachel, checking the ward, approved very much when she saw him taking it.

'Is his mother coming in?' she asked in an undertone.

'She'll come straight from school this afternoon, I expect. She's a teacher, you see . . .'

Rachel did see. It put her more clearly in the picture, but as Andrew was holding on to his grandmother's hand, she felt happier about him now. Maybe he was feeling insecure in some way.

Sister Mitchel returned from lunch and Rachel went to check the children from last night's accident. They both had leg and facial injuries and were content to sleep today away. Their uncle, who had been driving them home after a party for his children, was in the orthopaedic ward with more serious injuries.

When she emerged, Jonathan was at the table in the corridor, writing on duplicate forms.

'Oh, I'm so sorry—about Peter . . .'

'I know.'

She saw from his eyes just what the last half-hour had done to him personally. It was always like that, when they lost a battle. One was apt to forget the successes.

He stood up, gathering his papers in one hand as Sister Mitchel came around the corner. She too looked subdued.

'It's time you were gone, Sister Woods—your two hours off will soon go, you know, and you're here until eight, remember.'

'Yes. I hadn't forgotten, Sister.'

Jonathan had a few comments to make to her, then he caught Rachel up as she waited for the lift.

Neither spoke until they were on the way down, then he shook himself out of his frowning mood, squaring his shoulders while he drew a deep breath, expelling it slowly.

'You look tired,' she said softly.

'I didn't get much sleep last night—and today isn't proving one of the easiest, is it?'

'No' she said ruefully.

'What are you doing in your two hours off duty?'

'I'm going to phone this number actually. One of the nurses says her brother is changing his car for a bigger one. It's a Ford Fiesta and might be quite a bargain.'

'Well, do get expert advice, Rachel. You're an absolute greenhorn where mechanics are involved.'

'Could you look at it sometime, do you think?'

'Go and look at it yourself first and maybe we could go over tomorrow evening. It's my night off. Yours, too, isn't it?'

She wondered how he knew that as she went out into the dull wetness of the late October day. Unless he had taken a sly peep at the roster on the wall. But she was delighted that they would be together again so soon, her spirit lifting at once.

At four she was back on duty and Sister Mitchel went off until six. Four mothers were sitting with their children, which greatly helped the nursing staff. The children were given high tea at five o'clock and afterwards there was the usual routine to be gone through.

Later, Rachel, coming away from the sluice with a bedpan in her hands, almost bumped into Jonathan who was with Dr Roper, the houseman on duty. He went on to the end ward while Jonathan couldn't resist an amused grin, even though she noticed the rings around his eyes.

'So?' she asked defensively, 'what is so funny?'

'Not meant that way at all,' he protested. 'It's just nice to see you running around on this floor. Is Sister Mitchel back yet?'

'She's just gone into her office and is talking with Trina's mother. Can I help?'

'You know you can,' he murmured, leaving her in no doubt as to his meaning.

'Dr Paget!' she remonstrated, frowning a little, but

relieved that he had lost the defeated look she had seen earlier.

'Hadn't you better take that wherever it's desperately needed?' he suggested. Ignoring his banter she passed the pan to a junior nurse who came by.

'Marie wants this, Nurse. Ward Two.' And to Jonathan, looking through the window at the two children from last evening's take-in, she said seriously, 'Roger's X-rays are here. Would you like to see them?'

'Good.' He was very professional now. 'That elbow is going to prove something of a problem. He was in a mess when he came in.'

'He still is.'

Apart from a slight concussion, his arms and face had abrasions from a splintered windscreen and there was bruising and a leg fracture, and all this quite apart from his injured arm, now lying on a pillow splint packed with ice.

Jonathan studied the films, his brows almost meeting as he reached for the others to put on the screen.

'Have you seen these?'

Rachel nodded. 'Where does one start?'

'Or end? I think I'll ask Dr Winstone to see them. Just keep the little fellow as comfortable as possible for the moment—if you can. This ball is in my court, it seems, but I've never before attempted to reduce an elbow like that.'

'Good evening, Dr Paget.' He turned as Sister Mitchel's voice preceded her person along the corridor.

'Good evening, Sister. I've been looking at young Roger's X-rays. You've seen them?'

She nodded. 'I have. Shattered bone . . .'

'I'd like another opinion. I've written him up something a bit stronger for tonight so you can combat the pain for the time being. He seems to be coping—but then, I'll never cease to admire the resilience of these small fry. I'd also like another look at our asthma laddie.'

'He's a little better,' Sister said as she went with him along to Andrew's ward.

Rachel didn't see Jonathan again. She was too busy behind the curtains of one small girl who had just been very sick and was very much in need of a comforting shoulder to cry on, and a soft voice to go with it.

Later, when she returned from supper, Sister surprised her by commenting that Dr Paget looked very tired.

Rachel was putting some case notes away and looked up, feeling the colour creep over her face helplessly.

'Didn't you think so?'

'I didn't really notice,' she said in some confusion, because something in Sister's voice implied that she should have.

Her senior went on regardless. 'I was having coffee with Sister Theatre and she said there were two adult admissions during the night who he helped with, quite apart from Roger. The uncle is in Intensive . . .'

Rachel knew; it had happened while she was in Jonathan's room.

Sister Mitchel resolutely picked up a sheaf of papers and turned towards her office. 'That's it, you see. If you happen to be the resident registrar on duty and your pair of hands are the only available ones, it's your phone that rings. But Dr Hennessy will be back tomorrow. That should ease the situation a little also. We shall have Sister Bennett on days. So, all in all, the prospect looks a little better, don't you think? I'll get on with these.'

One thing Rachel *had* noticed—Jonathan was becoming very popular with the nursing staff. Of course, they had no idea that there was anything serious between herself and the Senior Registrar. As far as at least two nurses were concerned, it was a free for all. Especially Jenny Dee, who was not averse to a little slap and tickle, as she had expressed it to Rachel when they were both staff nurses.

Now Rachel was beginning to notice that Jenny usually managed to be somewhere around if Jonathan was. It was just something one ignored unless it got out of hand, but Rachel knew this wouldn't happen, at least where Jonathan was concerned.

The following evening Rachel left the sisters' house to meet him. She walked quickly out through a side gate leading to the road outside the hospital where they had agreed to see each other. It was a cold, starlit night but invigorating after the warmth of the hospital and she drew deep breaths of air into her lungs, feeling a delicious sense of freedom and release from the pressures and responsibility which now sat fairly and squarely on her shoulders. Perhaps when she was more used to her new status she would take it in her stride, but she found herself checking and re-checking everything now, just a little unused, as yet, to accepting the responsibility as she must if Sister Mitchel was absent from the floor. But all in all she was enjoying the new prestige, looking forward to getting stuck in once more to the reading she had set herself for the advanced papers she was interested in.

Jonathan's car nosed alongside and he reached to open the door for her.

'Oh, this is nice . . .' she said happily as she snuggled down into the seat and fastened her seat-belt. 'I was hoping that nothing would prevent you coming tonight.'

The car moved forward; Jonathan smiled tolerantly, as if he didn't feel much like smiling, or couldn't unwind as fast as she apparently had done.

'Nothing wrong, is there?' She was always quick to

sense his mood and tonight felt reticence, almost as if he had come out under duress.

His reply satisfied her, as it was meant to do, as he said lightly, 'Nothing that eight hours' sleep won't cure, I guess. By the way, you'll have to direct me. I'm not too sure of this district.'

'Oh, of course.' That was it; he was simply very tired. 'Yes, along this road to the roundabout, then turn right, keep straight on and it's the third turning on the left.'

She glanced sideways at his rather stern profile and decided to try and break his mood, if possible. 'I liked the car very much. I do hope I can have it. It's a lovely bright primrose colour and really a bargain, Jonathan, at the price. I hope you will think so.'

The car proved to be an excellent buy as far as he could see.

'But you should have a survey,' he suggested. 'No hidden rust . . .' She saw his mouth twitch at the corners.

So the sale was agreed, pending defects, and it was hers.

'I had only just advertised it the once and need a quick sale so that I can take delivery of the new one,' the man selling it explained.

On the way back Jonathan drove to the Green Dragon. Finding their corner seat unoccupied and their drinks soon in front of them, Rachel saw that he was beginning to unwind. He even admitted to feeling a bit uptight. 'Understandably, I suppose. We're none of us robots. Canada was so flexible, even though we worked hard. And then there was Inverness and that memorable fishing holiday and all that mountain scenery creating a general slowing up in every way. And then I went to Bath, and there were still no real timetable pressures. Then the hospital and the trauma of diving in head first to the change-over to a completely new wing. All of it's untrodden territory; you know how tough it is, Rachel, one's brain trying to keep pace with one's physical reflexes—or vice versa.' He shrugged. 'But still, it's nothing that a few undisturbed hours of sleep won't put right.'

Her eyes were more expressive than she knew and he looked quickly away when she said how much she appreciated his driving her to see the car tonight.

'Okay. You needed to get fixed up with another car. When do you intend going to Wales again?'

'Oh, not until my next long weekend.'

There was a polite coolness in his voice now which she was quick to notice, wondering a little how and why he could change moods so fast. This evening was not going the way she had hoped and when, after a lull in the conversation, Jonathan suggested they leave, she was first on her feet.

'Of course.'

'You've probably decided that I'm not very good at making conversation tonight,' he said on their way to the car.

'I understand,' she said quietly. 'It was nice of you to come to see the car with me.'

His face crumpled into a grin now. 'Somewhere I seem to have heard those words before,' he said teasingly, and she knew he was remembering her little red car and the garage in Scotland. At least it had lifted his mood slightly.

He kissed her briefly outside the sisters' house. 'See you tomorrow. Let me know what the garage people think about the car. Good night, Rachel.'

''Night, Jonathan. Get a good night's sleep if you can. See you . . .'

Why, she thought miserably as she went up to her room, were they behaving like this after that wildly passionate few minutes together in his room only hours ago? He certainly had a frustrating habit of blocking the natural development of their relationship. Once again Rachel felt emotionally insecure and wondered, not for the first time, if it was a good thing to be working again with Jonathan, seeing him every day, or not.

Next day proved to be a hectic one, right from the start. It was Mr Gerard's rounds morning, which meant getting ahead of the routine jobs as early as possible. Dr Winstone was coming over to look at Roger's elbow and give his opinion on the very bad fracture which had caused so much swelling and discolouration.

When Mr Gerard arrived and the retinue of doctors and nurses started on the long round of the wards, Rachel saw that Jonathan looked more relaxed this morning. And when he spoke to her it was in a purely professional guise, which she expected. Both Rachel and Sister Mitchel were consulted if Mr Gerard had a query or advised different treatment.

Nothing was hurried as they went from one bed to the next. Some small patients were told they could go home the following day. Others were not so lucky and fresh surgery was indicated or new medication ordered. Rachel felt very involved now and accepted her new status professionally, hoping to become as good a ward sister as her senior. Thankful, too, that she was lucky to have such a good tutor.

Jonathan was back again after lunch with Dr Winstone and Rachel attended them until a crisis arose over a new admission and she had to go and deal with it.

Before Jonathan left, Dr Winstone having already gone, he sought her out.

'Sister Woods? Can you spare a minute?'

'Of course, Doctor.'

Only Rachel saw the tenderness spring into his eyes as he looked down at her. For a moment her pulses raced; then she was listening intently.

'Dr Winstone will have Roger first on his list in the morning. Eight-thirty. He's going to put the arm in a traction splint and hopefully the reduction will hold. It is indeed a very bad fracture. But we'll do our utmost to get it reduced.'

Rachel had a few queries to ask before they were through and he went off down the corridor, his white coat tails flapping behind him, head bent, and in serious mood. Yet strangely she felt much happier as she went to answer the phone on her desk.

It was the little pneumonia boy's mother, asking anxious questions.

'Would you like to talk to his doctor, Mrs Walker?'

'Yes, I would, Sister. I can't understand the other thing they think is wrong with him.'

'I'll arrange a meeting and call you back.'

'All right, Sister. I'll wait here.'

Rachel tracked Jonathan down as he was leaving his office.

'Oh, sure. Ask her to come over and call me when she's here. Her husband too—if he can make it,' he added seriously.

Rachel loved the way his voice sounded on the phone. There was a closeness which always seemed to come over when she didn't have to be aware of the rest of him.

For the next week Jonathan came and went from the wards but, for some reason, she seemed to miss him.

Only when Mr Gerard visited could she be sure of seeing him, because Dr Soper and Dr Hennessy were the house doctors and spent most time on the wards when they were not in theatre.

Glancing from the office window one afternoon at her little primrose car sitting out there in the late autumn sunshine, Rachel saw Jonathan going across towards the neurological building. At the same time Staff Nurse

Jenny Dee appeared from the nurses' block, making a bee-line towards him.

Jonathan was laughing down at her, obviously enjoying whatever she had said to him. In fact they could have been having quite a flirtation out there in full view of everyone.

Even when they separated, Jenny kept turning back to look after him. There was just something about the chance meeting which Rachel found oddly disturbing.

She put it quickly from her mind when a trolley passed her door with a small girl back from theatre after a tonsillectomy. Neither did she comment when Jenny arrived back quite a few minutes late. Instead, Rachel asked her to help in getting the little girl settled.

'Afterwards, perhaps you could organise getting the two small wards ready for a fresh intake. The beds haven't been stripped yet and they've been vacated for at least three hours.'

'I thought Nurse Bray was doing them.'

Rachel raised her eyebrows but made no comment, and after checking the small girl in the bed, went back to her desk work which was bringing the report sheets up to date.

But the sound of a crying child took her swiftly to find out who it was. A few comforting words and a new set of toys from the basket in the corner were all that was needed.

In the bigger ward, four sets of eyes were watching the antics of Paddington Bear at the theatre amid peals of laughter, which broke Rachel's slight depression and she laughed with them.

It was Jenny herself who set the next set of doubts moving around her brain when she asked if she might leave right on time after supper.

'I don't see why not. We're well ahead tonight. I

shall be here and there will be four of you until eight. Something special on tonight?' Rachel asked.

'Dr Paget is giving me a lift to a lecture over at the teaching college. I happened to say I wanted to go and he decided to go along too. Only it starts right on eight sharp.'

'I see. You're going together then?' She was keeping her voice calm.

Jenny nodded. 'He's picking me up at the gate. It should be interesting . . .'

Nothing of the inner rise of disappointment she was experiencing showed outwardly on Rachel's features. She had so hoped they might have managed an hour or two alone tonight. She had known it was Jonathan's free evening.

In her office she stood with her back to the desk, fighting with her feelings. He is free to go where he likes and with whom, logic argued; but couldn't he simply have told her? What really hurt was that he either didn't think it important, or was deliberately playing around.

She was well aware how attractive the rest of the hospital staff at Great Cedars found Jonathan; she'd known that even before he went to Canada and he obviously felt that he was free to choose from among them if he wanted to. So where did that leave her? Perhaps the time had come to accept that Jonathan didn't want to be with her half as much as she wanted to spend every minute possible with him.

A knock came at the door and a nurse put her head round. 'Can you come, Sister?'

'Right now, Nurse. What is it?'

Almost at once Rachel had switched her mind away from Jonathan and went into the ward where a nurse kept watch by the little tonsillectomy girl.

'Call Dr Soper, Nurse,' she said at once.

'Not Dr Paget, Sister?'

'Dr Soper will bleep him if it's necessary. Hurry, Nurse.'

Rachel adjusted the drip, her hand going back to check the child's pulse, which began to steady. Everything stood ready in case of emergency. Rachel never panicked. In fact, in any crisis she usually felt very calm and clear-minded. Soon Dr Soper's footsteps sounded in the corridor and he came in and up to the bed.

The crisis passed and the wards settled down to another evening of low lights and gradual quiet.

When the night staff arrived to take over, Rachel handed over the report sheets and, after a conference with Night Sister, left a little later than usual.

It had been her first full day without Sister Mitchel. Even Sister Burnett hadn't been around today, having gone to have some dentistry work done.

Tomorrow would be better. It had to be, Rachel decided as she left the building and crossed the green under the trees to the sisters' house.

The huge clock on the tower showed eight-fifteen. Dare she allow her imagination to run riot over Jonathan and Jenny sitting in the lecture room listening to Professor Hilton's lecture? And wouldn't she have loved to be there to hear it herself?

Why hadn't she made the effort? Because ironically she had pictured spending the evening with Jonathan herself. But had she any right to do that? It seemed not. Didn't the way Jonathan had been in Scotland and that evening in his room give her that right? she protested, confused. So just where did she stand with him? Would he kiss Jenny in the car coming back and would she give more of herself—and no regrets? Perhaps.

Now Rachel hated her own thoughts and tried after that to shut them out. But they still came between her and the words and figures on the page she was taking notes from. The diagrams too—until she came to a page given over entirely to the Sculler-Christian Syndrome, a rare condition which had been diagnosed only three days before in one child and in which she had been specially interested. Jonathan too—in fact all the medical staff.

Absorbed in her study and notes, Rachel didn't notice the time until her eyelids dropped and her head almost hit the paper on her table.

Heavens—it is time for bed, she thought. She got up wearily and went to make a hot drink.

Her uniform was ready for next morning. She had already showered and wore her housecoat. She drew back her curtains and looked down on to a frosty moonlit scene. The trees seemed to be floodlit tonight and the whole world beautiful. One or two lights were on in the children's wing and slowly she raised her eyes to Jonathan's window. There a light was still on too. She wondered how long he had been back.

It was such a trite thing to get upset about—the fact that he had given one of the nurses a lift to a lecture. If it was so trite, why did she feel this awful sense of insecurity, as if the bottom had dropped out of her world yet again? Was she over-dramatising the whole thing? And yet once before, when she had refused to take Cheryl Summers seriously, Jonathan had simply gone away with not even a goodbye.

CHAPTER EIGHT

DURING the night the moon became hidden behind thick clouds, bringing rain and fog to the area. In the morning, as Rachel crossed over to the shrouded hospital building, it clung damply to the trees and even the lighted windows were only mistily bright. The dampness clung to her skin and already her hair curled in little tendrils around her face. She grimaced as a huge raindrop plopped down the back of her neck and wondered why she hadn't thought to pull up her hood.

'Not a very inspiring morning, Sister,' Dr Hennessy commented, catching her up and falling into step beside her.

'Well, it is November after all, I suppose,' she said bleakly as they entered the doors into the glass-topped corridor and comparative dryness.

'Has it got to you?' He eyed her half anxiously as they waited for the lift. 'No smile this morning?'

'Oh, it will pass. Didn't sleep too well. I hate this time of year leading up to Christmas.'

'Ah, that's another thing I wanted to talk to you about. We want some talent for the review.'

'Count me out, Jimmy. I've got a lot on my plate just now. Not this year. Sorry.'

'Okay. You'll have enough doing to keep the kids happy anyway, I expect. Oh, I must tell you this . . .' and he recited something really funny which had happened the evening before over a patient in Casualty.

As they left the lift, both smiling at the picture he had drawn for her, Jonathan was standing there waiting to go down.

Her eyes went straight to his, meeting them momentarily.

'Morning, Sister Woods,' he said briefly. Then, 'I've been looking for you, Dr Hennessy. I'd like a word.'

Rachel turned and made her way towards the small cloakroom off the corridor. She found it difficult to define the expression in Jonathan's eyes. It had certainly evoked some response from her heart on impact, she had to admit, but she dismissed him from her mind quite easily when she remembered that it was another nurse he had taken with him last night. Also that she had to do something about her vulnerability where Jonathan was concerned; sleepless nights had a way of becoming a habit and it just was not on.

So her expression was a little severe as she walked along the corridor past the first wards. Because these were open-plan, the children could see her and, in some cases, had actually been waiting for her appearance, shouting in unison, 'Hallo, Sister—come in here first . . .'

'Hallo, you noisy lot,' she said half chidingly as she went into the ward.

'My Mum brought this in for you.' A boy in the end bed held up a box of chocolates, his face one huge grin. 'It's for looking after me.'

'Oh, what a lovely surprise! Thank you, Eddie.'

'Aren't you going to open them?'

'I don't think so. Not before breakfast. Perhaps later. But thank you very much—what a nice way to start the day.'

She was soon caught up in the bed-making and on-the-spot decisions which evolved hourly, and the progress reports were well under way when Sister Mitchel called the nurses together and the format of the day was discussed.

Later, Jonathan came into the corridor positively

breezing along to his room, obviously in a very good mood as he went through his mail.

Afterwards, it occurred to Rachel that he deliberately chose to wait until Sister Mitchel went off for her coffee break before emerging to start his ward rounds, because the moment she had disappeared through the swing doors, he opened his door wider and called her.

'Can you spare a moment, Sister Woods?'

'Yes, Dr Paget.'

Perhaps he noticed the way her head went back and the cool, professional note in her voice, because he raised his eyebrows quizzically before asking in an undertone, 'Something bugging you, Rachel?'

'Of course not. I am rather busy though.'

'Mmm. Then we'll get on with the ward rounds,' he said briskly.

'I'll get the files.'

'Just one moment before you go. Can we talk sometime?'

She was off guard; he had caught her as she turned to leave the office.

'Tonight?' he went on. 'Come up to my room when you're free. I'm on call but will be there. You'll come?'

After a moment's hesitation Rachel answered, 'Yes, if it's that urgent.'

He opened the door for her. 'Shall we start at this end, Sister? I think we can let Andrew go home sometime today, don't you?'

Jenny Dee, coming out of the ward with a syringe in a kidney dish in her hand, gave him a wide smile which only brought a cool, 'Morning, Staff Nurse,' from Dr Paget. He reached for the notes Rachel was carrying and together they went in to the first cot, looking down at the small girl sitting up and patiently trying to put an arm back on to a doll.

At Jonathan's, 'Hallo, Mandy. What's happened

here?' she held the doll and the arm confidently up to him.

'I was taking off her pyjamas to get her dress on and it broke. I 'spect she wants a plaster on. Could you mend her?'

'Mmm—I think she'll need to go to the dolls' hospital for that,' he said cheerfully. 'Better let Sister take her along.' Meanwhile, he went over to the toy shelf and took another one, already dressed, bringing it back to the cot. 'Why don't you look after this doll while she's gone? She looks a bit lonely up there.'

Handing the broken doll to Rachel, he caught her eye for a moment, the lurking amusement deep in his own, as he moved on to the next bed.

Calling a passing nurse, Rachel said quietly, 'Put this on my desk, will you?'

The surprised nurse went off with the doll, but Jonathan was already concentrating on the new boy who was recovering after an emergency operation for acute appendicitis.

After a check of the relevant points and running his eye down the chart, he smiled reassuringly at the still apprehensive child. 'All over now, Terry. You'll soon be playing football again. You can go home in a few days, how's that?'

Oh, Jonathan . . . Rachel's heart cried, as she watched him. At times like these, I know why I love you so much.

She was excused then, for Sister Mitchel joined them, and she went off to help with some of the dressings.

Already feeling much lighter in spirit, the day, filled with routine tasks and some emergencies, passed very quickly and it was with some surprise that she heard Sister Mitchel reminding her that she was due to leave.

'It's after seven, Sister Woods.'

'Good heavens, so it is! Foggy, too, out there again.'

'Mmm. It usually heralds a bronchitis intake, so be prepared. I'm off tomorrow, you know.'

'Yes. Have a nice day, Sister. Good night.'

It was with rather mixed feelings that Rachel went up to the top floor later in the evening. While she showered and changed into a sweater and skirt, she had been reminded of Scotland and Jonathan's varied moods there. There were the times when he needed her, expressing his highest hopes and his frustrations in his work; proving too that he felt very close to her, both physically and mentally; that he trusted her, that she was very special in his life. But there were also those other times when he shut her out, seeming to delight in meaningless flirtations as if to keep her guessing. What, she wondered, was he trying to prove? Just how much a part of his life was she allowed to become? Just where did she stand?

Her tap on his door brought him immediately to open it and, as before, the room was bathed in a soft glow, welcoming, an inevitable part of him.

'Come on in, Rachel. I'm sticking to coffee tonight, just in case, but I've got it perking.'

'I could smell it out in the corridor,' she said laughingly, at ease instantly. 'You'll have everyone on the floor inviting themselves in.'

'They think I'm working and wouldn't dare to intrude. I've cleared the settee, so there is at least one comfortable seat in the room. Hope you hadn't got anything on.'

'Actually, I'd planned to do some work on my project, too.'

'Well, I suppose I could have phoned, but I wanted to do this as well.'

He took her in his arms then, his face expressing his feelings as he nuzzled her tenderly. 'Oh, I just love the feel of you in my arms,' he said huskily, 'it's like coming home.'

She felt submerged in the sensations enveloping her, melting the coolness of the morning, destroying all her doubts again as she responded to his kisses until they were both breathless.

'It's good to see you, honey, and without that starchy cap. Not that you don't look the part—indeed you do, and I'm proud of you. But you're irritatingly untouchable when you're wearing it.'

'Just as well,' Rachel reminded him, her eyes like huge, dark pools under the well-shaped brows. 'I must admit you do keep your professional profile very much to the fore. I'm relieved on that score. No one would ever suspect that you're the least bit interested in Sister Woods other than on a doctor-nurse basis. Now, some of the nurses. Well, maybe they are on the receiving end of a few flirtatious grins here and there—or perhaps accompanied to a lecture or two . . .'

'So that was the reason behind the icy approach this morning, was it? Surely not?' He brought her a steaming cup of coffee and sat beside her, eyeing her thoughtfully. 'Was it?'

'Not really.' She could afford to dismiss the whole thing now and wished she hadn't spoken of it. 'This is good.' She raised her eyes to his. 'Hadn't you better tell me why I'm here? Just in case you're bleeped.'

'Okay. Weekend after next,' he began without preamble, 'I'm off duty for forty-eight hours. Can you manage yours at the same time?'

'Actually, I'm due for my Friday till Monday. But I was going home.'

'Good. But maybe we could spend Saturday together. Or a part of it. I'd like you to meet my father and you can go on from Bath, can't you? What about lunch?'

'Well, I hadn't planned to drive down until Saturday morning anyway.'

'So you could still make it to the farm before dark? I've told him about you and he suggested we meet.'

Her heartbeats quickened. 'I don't mind night driving in the least, so there wouldn't be any desperate hurry. The roads are well lit; it's just the last bit that is only negotiable in dry weather. No problem.'

'Good.' He put his cup carefully back into its saucer as if deliberating about enlarging further. Instead, he commented, 'I guess we have to get right away from this environment, just for a short time sometimes. I did warn you that we could easily become submerged. Well, right now it's time to come up for some air. How about you?'

Rachel was trying to get a few things clear in her own mind, but with her hands imprisoned in both his, it was difficult.

'You're preaching to the converted,' she told him gently. 'I just know that I shall look forward to the break very much. Also to meeting your father. But won't your mother be there too?'

He let go of her hands then, frowning slightly before looking back at her. 'I have a stepmother. My father married again when I was around seventeen, three years after my mother's death. So I have a stepmother who I rarely see because, apart from other things, she likes to travel abroad a great deal, and a stepsister who I don't want to see too often anyway.'

'I'm sorry . . .' Rachel slid her fingers into his. 'You've never talked about your family—I didn't know.'

'Yours is a family, Rachel. Mine certainly isn't. My father is a fine man, but a rather private person. It's probably my fault that we are only now getting to feel closer.' He shrugged. 'But he does have a "keep off the grass" area where one doesn't intrude.'

'So his second marriage didn't work out . . .?' she asked pensively.

'You could say that.'

He moved a pile of medical journals absently, then brushed off his mood. 'More coffee?'

She shook her head. 'No, thanks. But I'm glad you told me about things at home, Jonathan. Now, let's make plans for the weekend. What time do you want to start?'

He made a grab at her. 'As soon as you like. Before that, if possible.'

The teasing grin was back on an otherwise serious face as he pulled her to him, but his kiss, long and deep, was broken by the ringing of his phone, forcing them apart reluctantly.

'Just as well,' he muttered, answering it at once. 'Okay, Sister. Be right down.'

'Not before you've got rid of this,' Rachel told him as she removed the lipstick from his face while her eyes danced up into his.

'Witch . . .!' He had already opened the door and they ran the last few steps to the lift as the doors started to close, until they slid back again, held by a registrar from the maternity wing who was still getting into his white coat.

'Hallo, Sister. Been enticing you up to his den, has he?'

'That's enough, Simon!' Jonathan growled warningly. 'Is there a flap on?'

'A couple of ambulances just came in. Your guess is as good as mine. I've got a mum in a hurry, it seems.'

On the ground floor they walked off quickly, leaving Rachel reading a notice on the board.

Oh dear, Christmas plans already. On the children's floor these were very important, and she supposed would have to be worked out soon; as yet, they were very tentative indeed.

Right now her own thoughts occupied her fully as she

walked along the path among the trees, thick with wet leaves, sadly losing their autumn colours now.

Surely, if Jonathan wanted her to meet his father it had to mean something? She could forget that last night he had taken Jenny to the lecture. It meant nothing. She had over-dramatised the whole thing.

Her lips were warm from his kisses. Oh, what ecstasy they evoked and how she loved that man! As she drifted into sleep one thing was certain; there was no other man she could possibly love half as much. So she would wait. Sometime, Jonathan would tell her what she most wanted to hear. She was already counting the days to their weekend away.

At the beginning of the week Jonathan was away for two days at a seminar and Rachel didn't see him again until the Thursday. Either Sister Mitchel was within earshot or another member of the nursing team on the floor, or he was preoccupied with some rather complicated cases involving other doctors, but it happened that she usually caught his back view disappearing through the door.

But on Sister Mitchel's day off Rachel did the ward rounds with him, and as they were going through the medication chart, Jonathan said quietly, 'Is nine o'clock all right for you on Saturday?'

'Fine . . .' Rachel was powerless to prevent the glow shining through as their eyes met, and he couldn't fail to see her happiness.

Staff Nurse Dee saw it too as she came out of a ward, pushing a small patient in a chair to the loo.

Fortunately for her peace of mind, Rachel didn't realise this. Nor that on Saturday morning Jenny, closing one of the ward windows, saw Jonathan's car nose its way into the tarmac drive and out towards the main gates, and noticed that in the other parking lot, Rachel's car had gone too. Yet she was sure it had been there fifteen minutes earlier. She put two and two together and came up with a supposition which did nothing for her mood the whole of that day, and the next, and at the evening meal she couldn't resist sharing her suspicions with her room-mate.

'Only don't say anything, Liz. I could be wrong, but it ties up somehow.'

All of which was quite enough to set the first bud erupting on the hospital grape-vine and soon growing into a full-sized grape, with the seeds tucked away inside it.

Jonathan caught up with Rachel's car and passed it just outside Marlborough, having kept it in sight until then. In the small county town they planned to stop for coffee. Rachel felt like a schoolgirl on a day's holiday, having made up her mind to enjoy every moment of this week-end. Especially today, which was all she and Jonathan would have together.

'So,' she queried as they sat facing each other in the Georgian bay window of a café, 'what plans have you?'

'Lunch with Dad at home around one, if that's okay with you?'

She was conscious of a thrill of pleasure. 'Of course it is. How nice.' Then a moment later, 'Who else will be there?'

'Just us. My stepmother is still in America visiting some of her family. Louise works in London and doesn't get down very often. Mrs Crabbe housekeeps and does the cooking. She and her husband have a flat in the basement. He does odd jobs and the garden. An arrangement that works very well, I guess.'

Rachel smiled as another of the Canadian phrases which he hadn't quite lost slipped out. Though there were so many questions she would like to have asked, she hesitated, not wanting to intrude too much into his family background unless he chose to tell her of his own free will. She sensed his reluctance to say too much and although she felt a natural curiosity, she was content to just enjoy being with him.

Jonathan was studying her now through half-closed eyes which approved of the way she looked.

'I like it . . .'

'What do you like?' She couldn't prevent the blush which crept over her face under his gaze.

'The way you look.'

'Oh, well, you didn't expect me to come to lunch with your father wearing jeans and a sweater, did you?'

'I just thought you would like to know, that's all.'

'You've seen this suit before,' she reminded him.

'I know. The heather colouring is right for you. Welsh tweed, isn't it? That ivory sweater, too. Perfect together.'

She smiled delightedly. Pure extravagance, she had thought, when she had bought it at a Scottish woollens shop in Inverness. It was the first cashmere she had ever possessed. But now, because of Jonathan's flattering remarks, worth every penny of her hard-earned savings. Like her parents, Rachel had been taught shrewdness where money was concerned, but also to appreciate quality too.

There was no sun today, which one hardly expected in November, but the town looked as beautiful as ever as her little yellow car followed Jonathan's down the long, steep road. Across the valley, the famous crescent of Georgian houses in their semi-circle, lovely reminders of the elegance of days gone by, were unaltered by time.

It was difficult now to keep Jonathan in sight because the traffic was building up, and Rachel was hidden for a short time behind a heavy container lorry. He had waited, however, and a little further on disappeared into a long street, turning off into a crescent where, here too, the character had been preserved.

She saw that he had drawn into the kerb and was getting out, locking his door. When she stopped her car behind his, Jonathan was there to open her door.

'Good driving, Sister Woods,' he complimented her. 'I expect Dad's around somewhere.'

They were in front of a tall terraced house, which had been lovingly preserved, colour-washed in palest blue with shining brass handles on the white front door. This, then, was obviously another of the preservation areas of this historic town. She noticed a brass plate beside the door, '*Dr R Paget*', but before she could comment, the door opened and Rachel was conscious of a nervousness she hadn't envisaged as she went up the steps to meet Jonathan's father for the first time.

He was tall, like his son, and—she caught her breath, because the same fascinating eyes, flecked just as those of the man beside her, were regarding her intently from under thick, greying eyebrows; his hair too, though sprinkled with a lot of grey, was the same texture and she knew just how Jonathan would look as an older man.

'Hallo there, Dad.'

He smiled down at them, not hiding his pleasure, and was suddenly younger.

'Nice to see you, Jonathan. And this is Rachel?'

He had grasped Rachel's hand firmly and was saying how glad he was that she could come. His voice had a West Country accent which endeared him to her right away, her nervousness already gone. In fact, as they drank dry sherries in the lounge before lunch, he and she established quite a rapport, much to Jonathan's obvious delight.

But Rachel noticed in an unguarded moment some strain around the older man's mouth and that his eyes held a depth of sadness at times, unlike his son's, which were sometimes teasingly alive.

Despite that, there was a happy atmosphere generally over their lunch, served by Mrs Crabbe, who was obviously a trusted member of the family and just as pleased to see Jonathan home as he was to see her again.

'You are staying tonight?' she asked him when she brought coffee. 'Your room is ready.'

'Oh, sure . . .'

His father asked in which part of Wales Rachel's parents lived, and now the conversation drifted to her home and the farm.

'So you're going on there today?'

'Yes. Later this afternoon, I expect.'

The phone in the hall rang insistently and Robert Paget got up to answer it.

When he came back he apologised to them both. 'I have to go out, I'm afraid. One of my private patients. I did promise that I would go if her condition deteriorated, although there is nothing more anyone can do now. She's just had her ninetieth birthday, but both she and her husband are friends of mine. You will excuse me . . .'

'Of course.' They understood that he had no alternative.

'I hope I'm going to see you again, Rachel, and soon. Keep my son up to that. Jonathan—you'll be here this evening?'

'Yes. That's for sure.'

Jonathan stood behind the voile curtains watching his father go through the garden to his garage. Rachel joined him.

'I didn't know that your father was a doctor too,' she said softly. 'I like him immensely.'

'He doesn't do quite so much now; but he needs his work. He also reads a lot and keeps up with the major changes in treatment of certain illnesses, medical science moving the way it does. He's become very interested in homoeopathy recently, too.'

'Really? Oh, I didn't thank him for lunch. Do you think you could apologise for me?' she looked crest-fallen.

'Yes, of course. He did have to drive off rather suddenly,' Jonathan reassured her.

Then, with an involuntary movement, he pulled her into his arms, holding her close against his body as he searched for her mouth, and during that long kiss every part of her sprang to awareness, her arms tightening around the back of his neck.

'Oh—Jonathan . . .' she murmured when he let her go.

He was breathing fast too, like her, thrown by the depth of feeling enveloping them both.

'Oh, Rachel! You're the only woman who does this to me,' he ground out throatily. 'You do know that . . . Come on, I'll show you around. Mrs Crabbe will want to clear, anyway.'

Rachel followed him up the curving, red-carpeted staircase to the landing above, then along to a room at the back.

'I still have my own room here.' He flung open the door. 'As you see, it's a kind of bed-sit where I can always come if I want to. Dad insisted on leaving this room as it was.'

'It's a lovely house.'

'Belonged to my grandparents. Dad was born here.' Jonathan stood back for her to go inside.

'It looks like you.' She was smiling at the photos of school teams on one wall. The plain furnishings were definitely him. On the mantelpiece was a photograph of a smiling woman and a boy of around twelve standing at a five-barred gate watching the sheep grazing.

'Oh, that's you . . .' She went closer, her voice softening, 'And your mother?'

He nodded. 'It was taken when we were all on holiday in Cornwall. Used to go every year to the same cottage. That was the last time. The next year it was France. And after that, I suppose I was off on school trips—Greece, the first time. So she and Dad spent their holidays together.'

'One does outgrow one's parents,' she said softly, turning to look up at him, close behind her. She had a much clearer picture of him now. But it had taken a very long time before he had opened the door into his private world.

'Why did you bring me here today?' she asked simply. 'Was it for a special reason, or just to meet your father? If so, why? You've told me so little up until now about your family that I am naturally curious to know why you've suddenly let me in . . .'

'Oh, Rachel,' he said, putting both hands on her shoulders. 'You simply have to have everything cut and dried, don't you? Does there have to be a special reason? Can't you just leave things the way they are?'

'I'm sorry. Don't be irritated with me. I just didn't quite understand, that's all. Well,' she had a sudden insight, 'perhaps I do, after all. And I do so want you to be happy. You see, I'm only completely happy when I'm with you. It's as simple as that—and I think you are too. But you seem not to want to admit it.'

'Of course I'm happy, as you call it, with you. Why else are you here? But happiness! God, it's such a transient thing one never really knows at the time. It's only afterwards that, if you're honest, you think—"I was happy then". You can't expect any doctor today to see things through rose-coloured glasses. It's a stark, cruel old world out there.' He shrugged. 'I don't see anything the way you do, I'm afraid. And certainly no permanence in relationships.'

'Ours seems to be moving along still,' she ventured.

'We don't *have* a relationship . . .' He grinned down at her, reaching for her again. 'Or do we?'

Flushed and with eyes shining too brightly, she at last broke away from his arms. Afterwards, she never knew how. She loved and wanted him desperately; but not like this.

They heard the front door slam and quick footsteps running up the stairs and, pushing her hair off her face, Rachel stood up and smoothed her skirt. Jonathan, too, was running his fingers through his hair, his brows drawn together in that hushed second before the girl appeared in the doorway, her eyes going from one to the other.

Rachel had an immediate impression of her even before anyone spoke. The expensive suede coat and boots to match; the neck scarf exactly matching the violet-blue eyes—and her hair; golden fair on her shoulders. She was certainly a lovely girl.

'I saw your car, Jonathan. Who's this?'

Her eyes had taken in the scene at a glance.

'This is Rachel. My stepsister, Louise,' he said, watching her. 'I thought you were in London.'

'Oh, come on, Jonathan, I always get back when you're home—if it's at all possible. You know that.' She turned to look at Rachel, her eyes hard. 'Are you staying?'

'No. I'm just on my way through to my home in Wales.'

'I see . . .'

So what has it to do with you? Rachel wondered uneasily. There was a hint of possessiveness in the girl's manner towards Jonathan as she picked up her overnight bag and threw a sharp look at him before going on to her room next door.

It was Rachel who got a queer feeling of being the odd one out, as she went with Jonathan down to the lounge.

'Would you like some tea before you move on?' he asked, but now his whole manner had changed.

'No, thanks. I can get some on the way. I—think I'll push on now and—please thank your father for lunch, won't you?' she said, very politely.

'Rachel . . .' he gripped her arm. 'Don't let Louise get to you. That is exactly what she wants.'

'I don't even know her, so she can hardly do that. Do you know where my things are?'

'I'll fetch them.'

He came back with her camel top coat over his arm and her gloves. 'I've got an idea. There's a small restaurant—on your way, actually. Have you been there? You get hot Sally Lunns for tea, dripping with butter. And good tea to go with it.'

'I've heard of it often. The oldest shop in Bath, isn't it? I haven't been there, but it's where they originated, isn't it?'

'Yes. Let's go now.'

'Why not?'

It brought an unexpected touch to the whole afternoon and as they sat in the upstairs room under the sloping roof and crooked walls of the tiny house pushed in between others in that old, historic street, there was an old-world gaiety about the silver teapots and hot buns dripping, as he had promised, with West Country butter.

'I don't know how I dare eat them after that delicious lunch,' Rachel commented as she poured more tea.

'And you with butter on your chin too . . .' He grinned.

So far neither had mentioned the appearance of his stepsister and, sensibly, Rachel decided to grasp the sheer enjoyment of the moment in the tea-shop, the warmth and glow of the table lamps and Jonathan's obvious pleasure at bringing her here, while outside the afternoon was already deepening into winter darkness and she knew she must leave soon.

'I'm not very happy about you driving there tonight,' he said, looking out over the rooftops. 'It won't be very pleasant.'

'I don't mind. I quite like night driving, and once I'm over the bridge it isn't too bad. Besides, it was worth every minute of being with you today.'

'You really mean that, don't you?'

'Do I ever say anything I don't mean?'

'No,' he said laughingly, as they left the room and went down the uneven stairs and out into the lighted streets, the shops already decorated for Christmas.

In the car park he kissed her again. 'Take great care,' he said simply. 'I'll see you on Monday.'

'You too,' she echoed lightly, taking her cue from him, although she hated to leave him now.

Yet something was puzzling her. Something she was not entirely happy about, as she drove along the motorways in Wales.

Perhaps the way Jonathan had withdrawn instantly the moment Louise had arrived had something to do with it. And also the possessive tone of Louise's voice when she spoke to him; her annoyance, which she hadn't bothered to hide, at finding Rachel with him. She had been positively rude, and Jonathan had said nothing. Not even when Louise said that she usually came home whenever he did. There was a strange little feeling somewhere inside, which Rachel recognised as a kind of instinct, not far removed from a feeling of apprehension. Oh, if only Jonathan were as open about everything as she was. Would she ever get to know and understand him properly?

Even today there had been the tiniest feeling that he was not being completely open with her. Was it simply that his father's second marriage had been a failure? Because that was the way it appeared on the surface. Why else would his wife choose to spend so much time away from him?

And the stepdaughter, Louise. Why had no one mentioned her over lunch?

That lovely house, like an empty shell; empty of love. Was all that why Jonathan refused to commit himself? Didn't he understand that physical love didn't last forever? It had to be the kind of loving to carry on long afterwards. The enduring kind. Perhaps he didn't trust a relationship that far ahead, but just how long could she herself go on with things as they were?

There was no immediate answer to that, and as she drove up the lane from the main road and saw that her father had put the powerful lights on for her over the farm buildings, Rachel felt an immense glow of happiness because this was home; and her parents had found the way to have a loving relationship that lasted through good times and bad.

They were both there at the top, waiting to welcome her home. Now she could really relax for the rest of the weekend.

'It was a long drive,' her mother commented. 'You must be tired,' she said as she went to bring in the meal from the brightly-lit kitchen.

'And so worth it,' Rachel told her simply, as she watched her take an apple pie from the oven and wondered how she was going to manage to eat again so soon.

CHAPTER NINE

SUNDAY passed all too quickly. In the morning, wearing gum boots, a thick sweater over her jeans and her mother's duffel coat, Rachel went with her father up over the grass slopes of the hills behind the farm to check his sheep, many already showing signs of being in lamb. Here and there, jutting granite rocks erupted from the uneven pastures. She knew them all and enjoyed the wind on her face as they stood looking out over the valley.

David Woods had a good rapport with his daughter, long ago having got over the disappointment of having no son to follow on. Maybe he had hoped Rachel might marry into a hill farm family and there would be a continuation of his land into the next generation. But she had set her heart on nursing and he was wise enough to let the dream go. Now, they talked companionably on several subjects as they tramped the hills together, and only he knew the intense pleasure it gave him to have her there by his side. His lovely girl, with the wind blowing her hair across her face and a far-away look in her eyes.

Was it of Jonathan she was dreaming? David was a practical man who called a spade a spade in his dealings with associates, and something about Rachel and Jonathan disturbed him. But, he decided, as he puffed on his pipe, it was not for him to intrude on her personal life. He just hoped that whatever bothered her would soon resolve itself.

That evening they sat around the blazing fire companionably, until he put down the Sunday paper and asked if he would see her in the morning.

'I shall be off to market early, Rachel.'

'Oh, yes. I'm on duty at one, so I must leave right after breakfast. At least I have a good little car now.'

'Yes,' he observed, 'you were lucky there.'

She had told them how Jonathan came to look at it with her. Also about yesterday's lunch with his father, but they hadn't commented unduly.

Except, 'We thought he might have come with you.' This from her mother.

'Oh, no. He had to be back tonight, anyway. Besides, his father likes to see him sometime, especially with his stepmother away.'

They hadn't known that his father was a doctor, and she didn't mention Louise.

'So when do you expect to be home again? No hope of seeing you for Christmas, I suppose.'

Rachel shook her head. 'Not this year. Maybe early in the New Year. We'll celebrate then, shall we?'

Next day, driving back along the M4 was no picnic. The traffic was always heavy on Mondays and all Rachel's concentration was needed, so that it was something of a relief when she at last turned off on to a minor road through the Gloucestershire hills.

She couldn't wait to see Jonathan again, and after the special moments they had shared on Saturday, the insight into his family background and meeting his father, she felt they had crossed a bridge to a much closer relationship. He had to admit to that, surely, even though there might not be many occasions when they could be together totally.

When she arrived on the wards punctually at one o'clock, having snatched a bite in her room, it was as if she had never left. One or two empty cots surprised her, but there were also three admissions, mainly with chest infections, which had turned nasty in the inclement weather conditions.

At the corridor desk, Sister Mitchel joined her as Rachel ran her eyes down the patient list.

'Oh, good. I'm glad you're back. I've had to lose Sister Bennet to the other section for today. Good weekend?'

'Really nice, Sister, thank you. Some new faces, I see.'

'Yes. They come and they go. The most we can hope for is that they don't come back,' she said briskly. 'Shall we do a quick tour so that you're fully integrated again? It's amazing,' Sister went on as they started to walk slowly away from the table together, 'just what can happen in a few hours on the children's wards. I want you to tell me what you think of this little chap in the special ward. He came in on Saturday after he had been seen by his GP.'

Bobby, seven years old and with tousled hair and blue eyes, looked very fed up with life in general as he lay, sweating slightly, his skin pale and clammy.

Sister explained his symptoms, listing the joint pains and that a blood test showed some anaemia, but that his throat swab had proved negative. 'Although he did have a very sore throat two weeks ago. Ring any bells?'

'Is there any rash?'

'Nothing too definite. A little redness on his trunk. He is a bit toxic, though there is only a moderate pyrexia. Dr Paget saw him earlier and thought he might be better in here. The pain has been very intense. He's on salicylates, of course.'

'Rheumatic fever, Sister?'

She nodded. 'Acute, he thinks. Mr Gerard may come up later to take a look at him. Complete bed rest and everything to be noted and reported. Impress this on the other nurses. I've had Nurse Grantley in and out all morning, but I think now we have to spare one of the juniors to sit with him. It's terribly important, as you know, to watch for any signs of carditis. Though it hasn't come to that yet and I hope it will not. We won't disturb him.'

Bobby was dozing anyway, his pain-killers making him drowsy. They moved away from his bed, careful not to jar against it because any movement brought an instant pain reaction.

'Try to get hold of the lab results before Mr Gerard arrives, if you can. I shall be back at four sharp.'

They moved on from ward to ward until Rachel felt completely involved again and began to wonder if she had dreamed up the whole weekend anyway.

But Jonathan's appearance, standing at the X-ray cabinet, fingering through the files, made the day come alive for her and her moments with him on Saturday certainly no dream. She couldn't leave the small patient whose damaged shoulder and arm she was in the process of rebandaging. The little girl who had been knocked from her bicycle was in great pain after her accident. But Rachel knew Jonathan would come looking for her if she was needed.

She heard his deep chuckle as he spoke to one of the nurses and a little smile curved the corners of her mouth. It had touched a chord in her memory, and she looked up, wondering if he knew she was the other side of the opening in the wall. But her expression changed when she saw that it was Jenny to whom he was speaking; his back was towards Rachel so that she couldn't see his expression. But she could observe the staff nurse, talking quickly to him, and saw the way she was looking at him before flashing her widest smile as she said, 'Thank you.'

For what? Rachel wondered as she finished her bandaging. They certainly weren't talking about anything to do with the patients and when Jenny picked up a report sheet from the table and went over to him again. she felt a prickle of displeasure. With a reassuring smile at the small girl, now comfortable against her pillows, Rachel went out and across to them.

Any patient information or problem should have been referred to her, so ignoring Jenny she said politely 'Good afternoon, Dr Paget. Can I help at all?'

'No, Sister.' He had picked the tension up at once. 'Just something Staff Nurse wanted me to know.'

'I see. Is Mr Gerard still coming to see Bobby?'

He nodded, avoiding her eyes. 'Yes. I'm waiting for him now, actually. Meanwhile, I've just seen Martin's pictures—have you had a chance yet?'

'Not yet.' Jenny, she noticed, was pretending to be looking for something in one of the drawers.

'Staff Nurse, will you bring Bobby's file, please, from Sister's desk. I think Mr Gerard is on his way.'

Rachel couldn't fail to see the way Jenny glanced at Jonathan as she went to fetch it, and as she had noticed that the staff nurse had been rather strange in her manner since returning from lunch, and even more so after Sister had left the floor, she did not feel entirely happy developing a situation which she would like to have avoided happening at all.

But there was no more time to reflect further because Jonathan was standing with his back to her, waiting as Mr Gerard, with two students and a houseman, came towards them.

'Ah, Dr Paget—I've brought these chaps along. Good afternoon, Sister.'

'Good afternoon, sir.'

'Well, let's have a look at this boy, shall we?'

Jenny handed Rachel the file and made as if to leave.

'You'd better come in too, Staff Nurse.'

Rachel inclined her head slightly as if to extract a reply from Jenny, who reluctantly mumbled, 'Yes, Sister.'

Now, even Jonathan had noticed and raised his eyebrows.

This—Rachel thought angrily—could not be allowed to go on, as she and the staff nurse followed up the rear of the entourage.

The first-year nurse sitting beside the bed got up at once.

'You can stay, Nurse,' Rachel said quietly, motioning her to stand behind her.

Mr Gerard studied the notes and then smiled down at the rather scared boy watching them from his pillow.

'Hallo, Bobby. Got a few nasty aches and pains, have you? Let's have a look, shall we? Nothing to worry about. We know you don't want to be prodded around too much.'

At the end of the examination he straightened up, explaining to the students the necessity for a bed cradle. 'Slight erythema marginatum, you may find sometimes. I'll go into that later. The history is very important in that case. Can we go along to your office, Sister?'

He had a lovely smile, Rachel decided, as she went to open the door for him, something which should have been thought of earlier by one of the others. Just one of those points of etiquette strictly adhered to at Great Cedars.

'Perhaps you'll take over, Staff Nurse,' she murmured to Jenny.

It was after the doctors had gone and Rachel was sitting at the table in the corridor writing up Bobby's case notes, because this was something Sister Mitchel was most strict on being done immediately, that she heard whispering and a giggle or two coming from the kitchen. She got up to investigate, expecting to see one of the student nurses helping the ward maid prepare drinks for the children.

Instead it was her staff nurse. Something was very wrong. It was quite out of context to find Jenny gossiping this way. What had got into her? Was she deliberately trying to cause trouble? And why?

'Will you take your break now, Staff Nurse?' she said quietly, even though she felt her anger rising as the ward maid looked from one to the other of them curiously. 'Rose can manage here quite well on her own.'

'I was going later today, Sister.'

'I prefer you to go now and be here when I go,' Rachel said firmly, turning as the nurse sitting with Bobby called her softly from his doorway.

'He says he feels sick, Sister.'

Rachel went immediately. Reaching behind his locker, she put a kidney dish at the ready. 'Ring if he is actually sick,' she said softly. 'I think it's probably a drug reaction. It will pass in a moment. Would you like a drink, Bobby? Carefully now.'

She put her hand under his pillow, raising him gently as he sipped some water.

Watching him discerningly for a moment, Rachel thought the nausea unlikely now. He was already closing his eyes sleepily again, as she gestured to the young nurse to resume her seat by his bed and tiptoed out, just as the staff nurse disappeared through the swing doors, having apparently decided to go for her break after all. It did nothing to dispel Rachel's feeling that she was up to something.

This kind of thing could not be allowed to continue and any other nurse would be reported; but Jenny was now a staff nurse and because Rachel herself had been one a very short time ago, and had been part of that scene, it made the situation a little more complex. She must give it some thought, fast. There had to be a reason behind Jenny's changed manner. Surely it could have nothing to do with Jonathan?

But this was not the time to let personal thoughts intrude. There was far too much to plough through right now. It must wait until later. Rachel had the whole evening to be by herself unless she accepted an invitation from one of the theatre sisters for a coffee evening in her room.

Dr Soper came then to give a transfusion to a child in the ward next to Bobby, and Rachel and he went along together. She didn't have time to leave the floor, even when Jenny returned looking a little sullen and off-putting, although she was a good nurse and very thorough in her work with the children.

Rachel's plastic apron over-dress didn't come off until all the children were safely tucked into bed. Then she finished her report and went round to check on them again, only speaking to Jenny when it was necessary.

Having decided later that evening that she would go to the get-together in Sister Theatre's room, she shelved her problem for the moment and went along around eight-thirty.

Just afterwards Jonathan phoned. As Rachel was nearest the door, fortunately, she answered it, out of earshot of the others.

'Rachel? Is that you?'

'Yes. Is anything wrong?'

'Why should there be? It's just that Simon's asked a few people in for drinks on Friday. Okay for you?'

He heard the pleasure in her voice as she replied, 'That's nice. Yes—I'd love to. I'm off at seven. What about you?'

'Should be my early evening. I'm working all day on Saturday. Good—I'll accept and pick you up around eight. Look forward to it.'

'Me too . . .' she said simply.

It helped her all through the next day, the fact that she would be with Jonathan again so soon. She liked Simon and his wife. He and Sally had only been married a year. Just after Jeff and Heather, in fact. So this was probably to celebrate their first anniversary. And, bless them, they had asked both she and Jonathan.

Thursday and Friday proved to be hectic days, with more comings and goings than usual. Every bed was occupied and the staff stretched to the limit.

Sister Mitchel was checking the coverage for the weekend. 'Staff Nurse is off tonight,' she observed, her brow creased, 'and Nurse Piper still has flu. We'll have to get a replacement from somewhere. And I can't have anyone around with the sniffles. Heard Nurse Grantley sneezing just now.'

It was debatable whether Rachel would get away by seven. Sister Bennet was acting as a liaison between children's wards and the special babies' unit. But Jonathan wasn't collecting her until eight, so she could just make it.

And punctually at eight that evening she was ready and waiting for him, wearing the violet dress he had liked so much at Gretna. Her dark hair shone like silk, her eyes large and luminous with the kind of happiness reflected only by a woman in love.

But at ten past eight they were looking a little anxious, and at twenty-past she wondered if she should call him.

Going to the window, Rachel saw that his room was in darkness. Perhaps there was an emergency. But surely he would have called her? From her tiny kitchen window she could see over into his car park, and yes—his car had started to pull out. She breathed a sigh of relief. It would help if she was waiting at the entrance downstairs.

She ran down the flight into the hall, across to the glass doors and out on to the step as it approached. But he was accelerating, and not slowing down. Amazed, she saw Jonathan, wearing his white polo-neck sweater—and, beside him, a girl. But she couldn't see her face—only a yellow scarf around her shoulders. Where was he going? Had he forgotten the day? Or had she got it all wrong? He wasn't even changed for Simon's party, for he would never have gone like that, in a sweater.

Rachel's heart beat furiously in a seemingly empty chest as she climbed the stairs again and went along to her room, grateful that she didn't meet anyone on the way. Disappointment and anger took over now from the joyous anticipation which had bolstered her up all day.

Throwing her coat down, she subsided into an armchair, then got up to go and check the time and date on her kitchen calendar. Friday. There it was, clear enough. It was Jonathan who had mixed the days—not her. But who was that girl? And where were they going? She must be from the hospital—one of the nurses perhaps. The yellow scarf, a wide one, was somehow familiar. Of course. Jenny wore a yellow one with her green coat.

'Oh, no,' Rachel groaned aloud, 'he wouldn't do that to me!' Tonight, of all nights, their first actual evening date for ages . . .

Should she ring Simon and apologise? That would be odd if it was she and not Jonathan who had got it all wrong. She was sure he said he was on duty all of Saturday. Sunday too.

It was just a dead loss. There was nothing she could do. Somewhere along the passage there was a burst of laughter and the high-pitched voice of another sister; then a door closed and there was a kind of silence. A lonely one; and Rachel got up suddenly, unzipping her dress and putting it back on its hanger. Then, slipping into a housecoat, she curled up in the chair again.

The hurt and disillusionment was too deep this time to be overlooked or explained away. Emotionally she couldn't afford Jonathan any longer. And especially if that *was* Jenny with him. That might account for Jenny's coolness when she had returned from Wales. Perhaps the fact that she and Jonathan were off duty the same weekend had lit a spark of small talk. Certainly there was an underlying resentment in the girl's manner. She was sure of that. But there was one thing she couldn't be sure about—had Jonathan simply stood her up in favour of Jenny?

Was that girl going all out to ensnare the resident doctor? Hadn't she carelessly admitted, at one of their nurses' evenings, that she liked sex, and if she wanted a man she usually got him?

Rachel got up then to switch on the nine o'clock news, forcing her thoughts away from the direction they had taken; but she was listening with only half her mind. The other part was still trying to fit all the bits of the jigsaw together, thought they didn't quite add up.

The film following the news held no interest for her either, and at ten o'clock she went to bed with a magazine. She felt physically very tired as she stretched her aching legs and feet in the soft coolness under the sheets, but her brain was not easily subdued and, even after her light was switched off, she wondered miserably what Jonathan was doing to her, and why. Which resulted in her not sleeping until the early hours, having to drag herself awake when the alarm pealed, and recognising at once the reasons behind her low spirits.

Besides, it was like getting up in the middle of the night. Outside, the lights were still switched on, the rising wind shaking the branches of the great trees as Rachel made her way bleakly across to the main building.

Puzzlement, which only Jonathan could answer,

clouded her mind. She must do something positive about clearing the whole thing between them. She must. And, somehow, switch off. There was too much responsibility waiting for her when she set foot on the wards to have any slip-ups. And, quite frankly, she had already asked herself during those lonely night hours if Jonathan, or any man, was worth all this anguish. She had been there before, and knew the outcome.

But, she sighed heavily as she left the lift, what am I going to do about it? How close they had been in that house at the weekend. She had felt certain, then, that he really loved her; that it was just a question of time before he admitted it openly.

But that was before Louise had come. More doubts crowded in. Why had she assumed that possessive, even rude, attitude? And why, she had wondered at the time, hadn't Jonathan introduced her as someone important to him? Presumably Louise would have been there when he got back to the house. What had he said then about the girl in his room? Rachel wondered.

Jonathan left the dining-room, where the doctors' meals were served, just in front of her. He seemed to be hovering until she joined him. She hadn't eaten much. With her head held high, she intended to prove that last night didn't matter anymore. But seeing him waiting there, his hair a little untidy and his eyes down-cast, she couldn't.

'Rachel—I don't know what to say. I've just seen Simon. It was last night, wasn't it? Can't think how I'd got it into my mind that it was tonight.'

'There's no point in saying anything now, is there?' Her whole demeanour was cool to the extreme. 'Sorry, Jonathan, I do have to get back. It was just a wasted evening, that's all. Obviously not for you though.'

She left him standing there, frowning. The confrontation had done nothing towards improving the misunderstanding between them one bit. In fact, Rachel now had to struggle with unexpected tears at the back of her aching throat.

But just before five that evening she went along to the sisters' office to look up a special phone number, and she was sitting copying it when she heard Jonathan's unmistakable footsteps in the corridor. They stopped at the open doorway of the office and he came slowly in.

'We need to talk, don't you think?' he said seriously.

'Yes, I think we do, Jonathan. But now is neither the time nor place, is it? I have an urgent phone call to make. Do you want to discuss anything else?'

'No. I think everything has been covered for today. Unless Dr Soper needs me for anything.'

He turned and walked out the way he had come, the swing doors grinding behind him. So, he had come purposely to talk to her then. Nurse Grantley, passing her with some clean bed linen, thought Sister Woods had an unusually worried look on her face this evening. It was very rare not to see that ready smile of hers.

Sunday was usually a quiet day at the Great Cedars Hospital. Something of the old atmosphere still clung to the day, even here on the children's wards. Casualties and emergencies were admitted, of course, but usually coped with by a depleted staff. Residents and housemen were on call. There were the Sunday papers on the adult wards and a service in the tiny chapel for those who could and wanted to go. Sometimes a choir came to sing hymns but not everyone wanted this. Even on the children's floor the visitors were more apparent and, well—Sunday was still Sunday.

Jonathan was kept busy and didn't come up to the ward unless he was needed. Dr Soper handled any routine decisions but usually these rested with Sister-in-Charge who, today, was Sister Mitchel, though only until after lunch. Then she was off until the following morning.

Rachel was kept busy all afternoon, answering queries from anxious parents, having to smile reassuringly and throw herself into the image she usually wore. And apart from looking paler than usual, she succeeded very well, being generally concerned about the small fry in her care.

It was only as she was leaving, having handed over to night sister, that the abject misery tucked away inside came to the surface. She was unaware of the dark night as she crossed to the sisters' house. Nor that her hands were cold because she had forgotten her gloves. Absorbed in her thoughts, she didn't see Jonathan until he crossed the grass under the trees towards her, gripping her arm firmly.

'Stop resisting me, Rachel. We have to get this thing out into the open. Let's go somewhere we can talk.'

'There's nothing to talk about any more, Jonathan. I know you weren't alone last night. I was waiting and saw you when your car passed. You're quite free to use your time any way you want, but be honest with me, for heaven's sake.'

'I'll wait in the car while you change. This is ridiculous,' he said irritably. 'Ten minutes, Rachel. I'll be by the gate.'

The urge to be with him was very strong, but still she hesitated.

'We can't just leave it like this. I'll wait in the car.'

'Ten minutes . . .' she said grudgingly.

'Okay, honey.'

And he's not getting round it that way, either, Rachel thought crossly as she went into the lighted building opposite. But in exactly ten minutes she was retracing her steps, hugging her loose plaid jacket close, hurriedly pulled on over a sweater and brown cord pants.

Jonathan leaned across to open the door for her, waiting impatiently while she fastened her seat-belt, a sure sign that he was irritated at even the necessity of an explanation of anything he did.

'Where do you want to go?' he asked shortly.

'It doesn't matter. We can stay in the car if you like.'

'I have to admit,' he conceded, 'that I prefer to discuss this in private.'

'Jonathan, whatever you come up with is not going to change anything, is it?' Her voice seemed devoid of expression, and now he glanced at her face, silhouetted in the street lighting. When he drew off the road, parking in a quiet spot, and turned in his seat to face her, his arm lying across the wheel, he asked impatiently, 'Now, just what is bugging you, Rachel? Is it because I muddled the dates or because I drove Jenny to the station?'

'You took her to the station?' she repeated tonelessly.

'Yes. She was late and might otherwise have missed her train.'

'Did she ask you to?' Rachel said slowly.

'Well, I had said I would. But yes—she did. She wanted to go home for the weekend. Afterwards, I came straight back and did a lot of work on my thesis. So is it because of Jenny, or because I forgot the right evening for us?'

'Both, I suppose,' she admitted.

'So you want the monopoly; is that it? Well, I'm afraid I can't commit myself to that extreme.'

'I realise that, Jonathan. So why are we here? What is the point?'

'Because my apology seems to mean absolutely nothing to you.'

She raised her eyes to his in the light from the dashboard and that from an errant moon up among the clouds. She saw that his jaw was set tightly with suppressed anger.

'You of all people should know that I loathe apologising for anything, Rachel. Least of all where I, in all sincerity, tried to help out another member of staff in a dilemma. If Jenny hadn't made that train, there wasn't another one until morning. You kept her late, apparently.'

She hadn't meant to, but now Rachel said furiously, 'Jenny went off duty promptly, as Sister Mitchel would confirm, purposely to catch the train.' Immediately she regretted it. But as she herself had taken over the unwashed children in Jenny's ward so that she could leave promptly, she bitterly resented his inference that the staff nurse had been kept late.

He looked at her consideringly. 'I had no idea you could be so churlish,' he said in a low voice. 'Neither do I intend having to answer to you, or anyone, for every decision I make, Rachel. Shall we get that point straight? Okay, so I confused the days for Simon's party, for which I apologised. But maybe it was not a bad thing if it emphasises this point. I am perfectly free to make any off-duty plans I choose, and so are you. You behave as if we are infinitely more committed to each other than we are. I have always insisted that I have no plans for a permanent relationship with anyone, and certainly nothing as soul-destroying as marriage. I hope this has cleared the air.'

'Yes. It has,' she whispered almost inaudibly.

'Rachel, I . . .'

'Don't.' Angrily she pushed away his hand as it covered hers. 'You are a philanderer at heart, Jonathan. You blow hot and cold, and you are most certainly free to have any relationship you choose. But please, don't include me in your future plans. I may have a few of my own.' He heard the sob in her voice.

'I'm not a saint. I admit that. I don't have to be. But a philanderer—that's something else, and I'm sorry you think that way. It's a bit much, coming from you, isn't it? I thought you knew the way I feel about you. But it seems you aren't exactly too clear about your own feelings towards me. I'll take you back now, okay?'

She nodded, not trusting her voice, and it was too dark on the country road for him to see the look of utter misery in her eyes.

This, then, was the end, even if he didn't realise it yet. But she felt as if the whole structure of her life had crumbled once again, and as before it was Jonathan who had knocked away the foundations.

CHAPTER TEN

IT WAS a long time that night before sleep finally blotted out the events, words and recriminations of that hour together.

When he stopped the car, Jonathan had reached over and opened Rachel's door, as if he couldn't wait for her to get out. She had left him with not even a goodnight and even before she reached the entrance he had roared off down the drive into the car park.

Monday morning lived up to its reputation for being the worst day of the week on the wards. The weather outside was dark and threatening and didn't help. The smaller children seemed unusually fractious and three at least were causing concern. Bobby was among them, still isolated and not making sufficient progress.

Sister Mitchel had problems of her own. She had never married and an ageing mother at home meant that her duties did not end when she left the hospital. She knew that she should do something about full-time care, but had put it off as long as she could, because her mother opposed it from every angle.

'I have my own career to consider,' she said. 'The present situation cannot go on but, other than a nursing home for her, what is the alternative?'

Rachel sympathised, appreciating the dilemma from a professional angle. She had nursed patients on geriatric wards and knew how traumatic and wearing some elderly ladies could be. It just wasn't fair that Sister Mitchel should have her life taken over this way.

But her own problems were not far from her thoughts

either. And the nameless ache in her heart was very real.

Tonight she would write to Heather and tell her of the decision she had reached in the early hours, to leave Great Cedars and try to find a post nearer to her home. She couldn't bear to see and have to behave normally to Jonathan, now that they were so far apart. No one could expect that of her. But neither was she able to give the real reason behind her wish to leave the hospital and the children's wards, where she had felt so fulfilled, knowing that it was the culmination of those years of training, right from that day she had made her childish decision to become a nurse.

As for Jenny, their differences and private affairs must be left out of the wards completely. And when the staff nurse reported back, Rachel asked her if she had enjoyed her weekend, quite deliberately setting the example.

Jenny replied that she had, and went off into the main ward, after they had gone through the reports together, to start getting one of the children ready for X-rays. When Jonathan came up after lunch with Dr Soper, Sister Mitchel went around with him, leaving Rachel free to help out the other nurses with the bed patients.

She had avoided even looking at him. He, in turn, was very involved. It was decision-making time for a few of the smaller, unpredictable children, in for observation.

Christmas was only three weeks away when he wandered into a room where some plans were being discussed. Rachel was one of those involved, at Sister Mitchel's instigation.

Jonathan sat down, crossing his legs nonchalantly, while he listened to what they envisaged doing on Christmas Eve for the children's benefit.

'And on Christmas Day, the parents, of course,'

Rachel said quietly, referring to her notes. 'The tree is no problem and we are already having presents handed in. But who is to be the Santa Claus this year?'

'I shall, of course,' Jonathan put in. 'Are we going to try getting everybody into the large room? What do you think, Sister Woods?'

'We can try.' Now she had to look at him, his sleepy-looking eyes regarded her quizzically from his chair across the room, stirring her emotions miserably. Rachel stood up.

'I'm sorry—you'll have to excuse me. I must get back.'

She left without looking at him again, but her whole being cried out to him and for him, and she knew she couldn't bear the distraction he caused her whenever he appeared.

Her mind was finally and irrevocably made up that same evening when she saw Jonathan waiting in the car park, standing beside his car under the lights around the outside wall. Her heart lurched. Was he waiting for her? Picking up from that morning's recognition of each other again?

But another girl was making her way through the puddles towards him, her yellow scarf blowing in the wind.

Rachel stood quite still under the trees. They hadn't seen her. So—they were dating now. She had to admit that Jenny was a very pretty girl, full of a *joie de vivre* that most men would find attractive. She believed in living for the moment, making up in her off-duty time for the strictness and privations of her work.

It hurt, the pain deepening as Rachel went across to the sisters' building. Was Jenny willing to simply have a good time with no regrets? And was Jonathan quite happy to go along on that basis too?

It had nothing to do with Rachel any more. She had

had her chance with him. Only she hadn't wanted his love on that basis. But perhaps he was not capable of the real depth of loving she needed and had been willing to wait for.

Tears stung her eyes; tears of resentment, of unbearable longing for the feel of his arms around her again. For the closeness of their bodies, the warmth of desire and the expression she had so often seen in those yellow-tinged eyes, which sought to hide his true feelings. All these she missed terribly now, but her tears were not of regret. She still felt that she had been right to wait for him to say that he loved her. Apparently he hadn't, after all.

Well—now it was too late. She would never hear him say those words now. It was over. What might have been was gone . . .

That same evening she looked carefully through the current vacancies in her nursing magazines. There were two which she actually thought she might apply for. One at a small hospital on the Welsh borders and another wanting a Sister-in-Charge of a baby unit with experience as a junior sister, here in Gloucestershire. It seemed an omen. Rachel sent a letter of application the next morning, before she could change her mind. Much as she loved being at Great Cedars, especially now, the time had come to make a change.

No one would understand her decision to leave. Not Sister Mitchel, nor Matron, nor any of the nursing staff she enjoyed working with. But she could not work in the same building with Jonathan without being completely destroyed. She was too deeply emotional for that; too sensitive to him as a person. And he was here, working and researching and fulfilling his own potential, carving out his future. Therefore it was she who must go.

Rachel told no one of her decision until she received a reply to her letter and, even then, drove off for her appointment without explaining why she wanted that particular day off.

But next morning she admitted to Sister Mitchel that she had every hope of taking up a new appointment. 'Quite soon, I'm afraid.'

'Does your decision have anything to do with Dr Paget?' It was unexpected and not quite the reaction she had predicted.

'Why should you think that, Sister?'

'Sit down. I've noticed that he is dating our staff nurse quite a bit. It was apparent at the end of term evening at the medical school the other night. I had to go because Matron asked me to, and Jenny had been attending one or two lectures, I believe. She and Dr Paget were together quite a lot . . .'

'But what does that have to do with me?'

'I think we all rather expected to hear that you and he had something rather special going. Or don't you listen to the grape-vine rumblings? You see, I'm not such an old maid that I can't recognise, and interpret, the way two people look at each other. Nor the way your colour rises when he appears, professional as you both were while on duty. He used to call you, wait for you—what happened? Sister Men's Medical saw you having tea at Sally Lunn's in Bath during that weekend you were both off together. So what on earth has gone wrong?'

'Don't ask me, Sister. It's just that we have no future together, it seems. And I can't stay here—I have to move on.'

'Well, I'm terribly sorry—and Matron will be too. I wonder what Dr Paget will have to say. Does he know yet?'

'No,' Rachel said firmly. 'And I do trust you not to tell anyone outside this room. Please—not yet, Sister.'

'If that is what you want of course, I won't. Is there no way we can make you change your mind?'

'No. I'm sorry. I have to go. The appointment is for January, so I shall have to tender my resignation this week, I suppose.'

Sister nodded. 'I am very, very, sorry,' she said sadly. 'But the work must go on, and . . .'she glanced at her watch, 'we don't have too much time before Mr Gerard will be here. Thank you for telling me.'

'Thank you, Sister.'

'For what?' she added, as they left her office together. 'Letting you go so easily? Perhaps I understand how you feel at this time—and I can see you have no alternative. So why make it harder?'

Christmas week passed quickly. They were busy, although only emergency or very necessary cases were admitted. A long letter from Heather brought back the memories vividly to Rachel's mind of that early autumn holiday, when Jonathan seemed so different.

Heather wrote that they were both very disappointed that things hadn't worked out. *Marriage can be such fun, with the right person, and we had hoped to have you both here again in the spring. Besides, I want you to get acquainted with your adorable godchild. Even if it was by proxy. And many thanks for the cuddly elephant. Ewan is going to love it. Come up any time you have the inclination, the time and the money, Rachel. Write and tell me about the new hospital. The amenities sound terrific and a whole new lot of people to get to know. Who knows what's round the corner for you?* Who knows? Rachel echoed.

The wards were decorated and hundreds of balloons festooned the ceiling. Even the tots were kept amused by simply watching them moving in the warm air. Christmas Eve was great fun, the little faces all agog as the nurses paraded with their candles singing carols around the wards. The tree looked gorgeous, dripping with parcels and decorations, and Jonathan was in and out whenever he could spare a minute.

Next morning the cots were smothered in festive paper as the presents and toys were unwrapped, the staff even busier than normal, keeping everything under control.

'I'm glad I was here today,' Rachel said to Sister as they watched the scene.

'Thought I should warn you,' Sister said, her eyebrows raised a little, 'but there is a whisper afoot that you're leaving, you know.'

'But how?' Rachel asked.

'I don't know. Not from me, certainly. But even in the most leak-proof buildings the walls have ears. I've always said so.'

Matron had agreed to replace Rachel at the end of the first week in the New Year.

'Which means you'll be here for the staff's New Year dance,' Sister Mitchel observed. 'Make the most of it . . .'

Rachel glanced at her quickly, but Sister said no more and went away immediately.

'What, I wonder, did she mean by that?' she mused as she waited for Jonathan to appear in his traditional Santa Claus outfit, complete with beard.

Excitement mounted and when he came in, with the list of names and presents to be cut from the tree, there wasn't an ache or pain in the room. At least, not one that made itself known. Eyes shone and voices shouted, and everyone, just everyone, was happy.

'Want to see you later,' he muttered under his breath as he put the first book into her hands, followed by an animal board game.

She started, meeting his eyes behind the shaggy white edging to his red hood. The next time she came back for more, he said throatily, 'By the main gate, at nine —tonight.'

'It's Christmas . . .'

'So what?'

She hadn't said she wouldn't go, but Sister Mitchel had asked her to go over to her home, a ten-minute car ride, for a drink. So how did she get out of that? Maybe, if she explained, Sister would understand.

Jenny and Rachel took turns at delivering the presents, after which there was lunch and a rest period and parents. The day flew by and when at last she had handed over to the night staff and made her way back to her room, it was eight o'clock. Here and there were sounds of some gaiety, but mainly it was quiet.

Jonathan was waiting and as Rachel joined him he had the car door already open for her. Immediately producing a sprig of mistletoe, he leaned across and kissed her lightly.

'My Christmas kiss. I didn't push it on the wards, in case you objected, though I must say the other nurses seemed to enjoy it. Even Sister Mitchel.'

'Oh, Jonathan,' Rachel groaned, half smiling, yet inwardly weeping because he was here, so close, yet now they were worlds apart.

'It's Christmas, Rachel,' he said again. 'Time for goodwill and all the rest.' He became serious. 'I've promised to see someone at ten.'

'And I've broken a date too,' she said a little crossly, because they were not getting anywhere and this was just piling on the agony—a sheer waste of time. His aftershave wafted cleanly over to her nostrils—which made it all so much worse, the division between them too strong. She no longer knew him. 'What is it, Jonathan? Why are we here?'

'There is a rumour, which can't be true, of course, that you are leaving Great Cedars. I just want to hear you deny it, so that I can discount it,' he said easily.

'But it is true, I'm afraid. I've already applied for another post.'

For a moment he regarded her as if he couldn't believe it. Then he shrugged, but she knew he was angry.

'What the hell is behind all this? You can't leave here. Those kids need you. It's your niche, Rachel. Why didn't you say one word about this to me?'

'I don't think it concerns you, Jonathan, any more. Neither do I want to discuss it. I've made up my mind, so that's it.'

'You won't go when the time comes—you can't.'

'We'll see, shan't we? Meanwhile, I have someone else to see,' she said coolly. 'Please let me out of the car.'

'Okay,' he ground out. 'Some Christmas this has turned out to be . . .'

Rachel had meant to tell him that she had received a Christmas card from his father. It had shaken her to see his signature under the greeting. Robert Paget. But just now, she couldn't trust her voice to hold out.

'Goodbye, Jonathan.'

She didn't hear his reply, only the sound of the engine as he drove off, the red lights at the back disappearing into his parking place. He couldn't suspect that her bravado vanished with him and that in three minutes flat she would be crying her eyes out alone in her room, her emotions released at last because this time it really was goodbye.

The New Year staff dance was on the third of January. Rachel had gone under protest, at Sister Mitchel's instigation. Well, it was the last social occasion for her at Great Cedars, so why not?

She hadn't expected Jonathan to be there. He didn't

usually attend these things and she was dancing with Dr Hennessy when she first saw him, already on the floor.

Her partner had noticed, even felt the involuntary tightening of her hand on his shoulder and the way her fingers clenched his. It didn't take him long to guess why.

'Jonathan's dancing with the new sister from ophthalmics. Have you met her? Very classy.'

Rachel shook her head. 'I haven't seen her before, but I heard she'd moved in two doors from my room. She's very attractive.'

'Trust our Resident to choose 'em,' Dr Hennessy teased. 'I shall try my hand in that direction in a minute, I think.'

The dance changed to an Excuse Me. It happened so quickly, Rachel's transference from Dr Hennessy's arms to the more familiar ones belonging to Dr Paget, that she had no time to catch her breath before she was swept into a strong and close embrace which almost forced the rest of her breath from her body.

'No partner, Sister Woods?' he murmured into her ear. 'That does surprise me.'

'I'm only here because Sister Mitchel asked me to be. I've got rather a lot to do tonight.'

'In what way?' he asked absently, his eyes moving around the room above her head.

Jenny had come in with two other nurses, bubbling over as usual with the kind of effervescence most men are attracted to. Rachel guessed they had already had a few drinks at the improvised bar in the office next door and she envied her staff nurse at that moment.

Already Jenny had searched the room for Jonathan and now, seeing him moving slowly to the music with Rachel in his arms, her smile faded for a moment or two as she watched them.

Rachel left the floor when the music stopped, even

though Jonathan followed her; she still moved on through the small groups either sipping drinks or eating from the buffet in the corner, grabbing her wrap from a hanger.

'Rachel . . .'

She disappeared into the powder room, which was empty at first, pressing her knuckles to her mouth, trembling still from the warmth of his body against hers, the feel of his cheek touching her face momentarily, the way his fingers had curled into her hand so naturally.

'I can't take it . . .' she groaned and, going through to a door at the back, she deliberately made her way along a corridor and out of a side door, and across to the sisters' house.

Long after the dance had ended and quiet prevailed outside in the grounds of the hospital, she lay there, staring up at the ceiling.

This was her last night at the Cedars. Yet he hadn't mentioned it. Well, what had she expected? A miracle? Not from Jonathan; he would never accept that he could be wrong. If he had once said that he was in love with her, and her alone, she would not be leaving here. She hadn't expected marriage. Not yet, anyway. But she did need total commitment from the man she loved. It was as simple as that. Trust and loyalty—they were what really mattered most. Jonathan could not concede either, so tomorrow—or today, actually—she was going out of his life. And, hopefully, the time would come when he would be gone from her own. More than ever now, she knew she was doing the only possible thing in moving on to pastures new.

But there was no comfort in the assertion. Maybe, in time, there would be.

And in the morning, as Rachel looked bleakly around at her room, devoid of her possessions which were now all neatly packed in her bags, she slipped into her uniform for the last time. She had to see Matron and tie up a few loose ends before vacating her room, and there were the final goodbyes to be said to a few special people, especially the children, which she had no intention of prolonging. Her replacement had already taken over and Sister Mitchel would be busy with her.

Jonathan was already in theatre, she discovered, and would be doing his rounds later in the day.

So Rachel finally drove her car through the gates of Great Cedars for the last time as lunch was being served on the children's wing. She felt nothing now except a heaviness in her chest, too solid to be released. This was the moment when she must start leaving it all behind. In two weeks she must be ready to take over her new post. There would be new babies to hold and nurse back to health. New roots to put down. That was the way to see it. It had been her own decision, after all.

It was late afternoon when she drove up the winding lane to the farmhouse tucked into the hills. Darkness was already enveloping the surrounding countryside although it was not yet four o'clock. Another world—which she hoped would bring peace and rest for her tired mind and body. Emotion, especially suppressed, as hers had to be, created havoc in sensitive people, she knew. Well—now it was behind her and it was up to herself to get over it all.

But that night, as she stood at her window watching the dark clouds drifting over the moon, she wondered what Jonathan's true reaction had been when he realised that she had gone. He just hadn't taken her leaving seriously. Or he had chosen to ignore it. Well, it no longer mattered any more, either way. It *must* not.

Her father's forecast was proved right and next morning saw the first snowflakes of the winter falling gently and soundlessly over the high ground.

By afternoon the world outside was white. 'If this continues, I'll have to get the sheep down from over the hill,' her father said worriedly. 'If it starts drifting, they'll be in trouble. But it is easing off now. I'll wait till morning. Maybe it'll turn wet and be cleared away by then. Never get them rounded up now, it's dark anyway.'

Her parents had accepted her decision to leave Great Cedars and after the first tentative questions, respected her reticence to talk about it. They both secretly thought that it must have something to do with Jonathan.

'It will be nice to have you home for a week or two. You look as if you can do with a few nights' good sleep,' her mother said, eyeing Rachel discerningly.

'I think that sounds like heaven,' Rachel replied, and they both heard the tremulous note in her voice and wondered why she had made such a sudden decision. But no one mentioned Jonathan.

Next morning she awoke to sounds of sheep bleating and more activity than usual outside in the pens. She was a farmer's daughter and knew what it meant. Snow.

Pulling on the warmest things she could find, including thick corduroy trousers, Rachel ran down to the kitchen where her father had just come in for breakfast.

'I've got some of 'em in,' he was saying. 'But the rest will need some looking for up there in the hills. Can you cope with the milking, Becky?'

'I'll help, Dad. What can I do first?'

'Have to get them in, lass. There's more snow forecast. Some of my best ewes are up there. Trouble is, you never know how far they've wandered. They'll be in the crevices and under the rocks—anywhere. I must get 'em down before dark.'

'Okay. We'll go up after breakfast then.'

Her father grinned. 'We will that . . . I see you're already dressed for it.'

'Take my duffel coat and boots, Rachel. I'll pack you a flask of soup and some sandwiches. Let's hope it doesn't get any worse,' her mother insisted.

But it did. All day the sheep were driven down from the hills and the conditions worsened. Although the hill farmers were used to this, and most prepared for it, they all waited until the snow actually came before bringing their flocks away from the green pastures.

For the fifth time that day Rachel climbed exhaustedly up among the drifting snow-covered rocks to find any stray sheep. This morning's search had produced a few surprises. Lambing had begun early for two of the ewes and there just might be more in trouble.

'Best get back down below now, lass,' David Woods said wearily, wiping the snow from his eyes. 'There's not too much light left. We've done our best . . .' He shaded his eyes against the blue-white glare of the virgin snow. 'There's somebody coming up. Can't see who it is though. A bit too late if he's come to give us a hand.'

It was not until the man came over the brow of the hill that, with a little cry, Rachel recognised Jonathan's snow-flecked face beneath the hood of her father's old weather coat. He was plodding through the snow in rubber boots, two sizes too large, his hands inside a large pair of sheepskin gloves.

'Jonathan!'

Only her father heard the sob in her voice and he wisely said nothing as she clambered down to meet him.

'What are you doing here?' she asked through half-frozen lips.

'Looking for you both. Your mother was getting worried. Are you okay?'

Her father spoke for them. 'We're fine, Jonathan.

Thanks for coming up but things are all under control, I think. Watch that drift there—it's deceptive. Rock underneath which could give you a nasty gash.' Tactfully he set off down to the farmhouse.

Jonathan was holding fast to Rachel's hand and now he flung an arm around her shoulders, ignoring the tears on her lashes, soon covered by snowflakes anyway.

'I should have been here earlier but the road conditions are appalling. Your mother has offered me a bed for the night so you'll have to put up with me, I'm afraid. Just as well. There are a lot of things to get cleared up, it seems.'

'I can't believe it . . .' Rachel gasped. 'I'm not dreaming, am I? What made you drive through roads like that?'

'You still don't know?' They had arrived at flatter ground now, although the snow was deep. With a desperate movement, Jonathan pulled her into his arms, looking down into her face. 'Because I knew the moment you had finally gone out of my life, Rachel, that you were too much a part of it, and without you, nothing else worked. I think, in a strange way, I grew up. I honestly don't think I could handle my own emotions until then.'

In the kitchen of their home, her parents looked out through a snow-clogged window at two people who had forgotten them. Etched against the white hills, Rachel and Jonathan were locked in each other's arms, oddly grotesque in their borrowed clothes. It was a revealing moment and David spoke first.

'He seems to be in love with our girl, after all, Becky,' he mused, a far-away look in his eyes. 'Wonder what went wrong?'

But Rachel knew already as, for the first time, the words she most wanted to hear burst from Jonathan's lips. 'I love you. I'd come to the ends of the earth for you—surely you knew that?'

'I do now . . .' she said, through chattering teeth.

But it was later that night, when her parents had gone to bed and outside the quiet of a snow-covered valley was broken only by an occasional sheep's bleat, that Jonathan admitted to needing her in his life too.

'Without you, it's kind of meaningless, honey. If I analyse the reasoning behind not wanting to feel committed, I find it goes back to my home life. My father was never able to do the medical research he wanted and, after my mother died, his re-marriage was a disaster; it all made me determined to steer clear until my own future was established, and not get side-tracked. Until you came. Even then, I almost gave in at Gretna. I don't know how I got out of that room without asking you to marry me right there.'

'I wish you had told me all this before,' Rachel said softly, as she gazed up into his face from her curled-up position on the rug in front of the crackling logs. 'I would wait for ever, if you asked me. I just wanted to know that you loved me as much as I loved you. I can still wait.'

'But I don't think I can,' he said tenderly. It brought back a scene in the cottage room in Scotland, as he gazed down at a new-born baby. This was the man behind whatever mask he chose to wear; the man she would always love.

She couldn't sleep for sheer happiness in her room under the eaves, as she went back over the things he had said to her that evening and the plans they discussed.

There were no more doubts. She knew, as she had probably always known, that Jonathan loved her. The barriers were all removable ones now they were out in the open.

There would be times when he might seem shut off from her. This she accepted, because he was a private person; separate and, like his father, individualistic.

But to be loved, and to know that, was enough—and more.